DENZIL'S GREAT
BEAR BURGLARY

Sherryl Jordan

19. 10. 97.

Other Denzil Misadventures

The Wednesday Wizard
Denzil's Dilemma

DENZIL'S GREAT BEAR BURGLARY

Sherryl Jordan

MALLINSON RENDEL

First published in 1997 by
Mallinson Rendel Publishers Ltd.
PO Box 9409, Wellington, N.Z.

© Sherryl Jordan, 1997

ISBN: 0-908783-26-4

Cover design: Trevor Pye

Typeset in 12/15 pt Century Old Style
by Cuthbertson Graphics, Wellington
Printed by Colorcraft, Hong Kong

Contents

1 *When Pigs Fly*

rouble was something Denzil was used to. He lived in trouble; it shadowed him, tracking him like a barn cat trailing a mouse, pouncing when he least expected it – usually just when he thought he'd been particularly clever. Always he had managed to talk himself out of the trouble – or to wriggle out of it by magic – but this time was different. This time the trouble was so huge, so devastating, that Denzil's career as a wizard's apprentice was in grave danger of being terminated.

It all began one fine winter morning, with an innocent request, and ten little pigs . . .

"I need to borrow something," Denzil said to his master, the great wizard Valvasor.

Valvasor was busy. "What?" he asked, impatiently.

"Your ceremonial robe," Denzil said. "I really need it, Master. Can I have it? Please?"

"When pigs fly," Valvasor replied.

"Does that mean No?"

Valvasor leaned over the herbs scattered across the ancient table, and picked up a dried branch with faded silvery-green leaves. He plucked off five leaves,

7

spread them on the table in front of him, and scratched words on them with a thorn. Then he wrapped the leaves carefully in a piece of muslin cloth, which he tied with a scarlet ribbon.

"I don't really know that all this is truly effective," Valvasor muttered, putting the bundle aside and beginning to prepare another. "But the women seem to think it is, so long as the thing is prepared by me. What are you waiting for, lad? I thought you were going to the village fair."

"I am, but I want to look my best," said Denzil.

For the first time in several days, the wizard gave his apprentice a long, hard look. "Good Lord!" murmured Valvasor. "When did you last mend your hose, lad? You've got twenty holes in them, below knee level! Goodness knows how many holes they have, higher up. And why on earth is your hair grey? What did you do – fall in the flour bin? And that looks suspiciously like raspberry jam oozing through your pocket. Have you been stealing the baker's pies?"

Denzil gulped and went red. "Not exactly," he said, shaking his head violently and sending clouds of flour out of his unruly black hair. "I just happened to be at the baker's, when the cat chased me. I hid in the flour bin."

"I didn't know you were afraid of cats."

"I am – when I'm a mouse," said Denzil.

"I see," said Valvasor. "A mouse in the baker's is the same as a thief."

"Burglar," said Denzil quickly. He hated the word thief, burglar was a far better title, more important and dignified. "I was a burglar."

"That's nothing to be proud of. You're supposed to be a wizard. You're supposed to live up to the honour and dignity of your calling, not go around falling into flour bins and looking like an animated scarecrow."

"That's why," said Denzil, wringing his hands pleadingly. "I really need it, master."

"Need what?"

"Your ceremonial robe, the one with rainbows and silver stars and glittering suns. I promise I'll take care of it. I won't let it drag in the mud, and I won't spill apple cider on it, or get toffee apple all over it, and – Oh, lord – just let me wear it to the fair, and I'll be good forever. I promise. I swear it."

"I gave you my answer," said Valvasor, bending over the herbs again.

Denzil stuck out his tongue, very quickly, and made for the door.

"Wait!" called Valvasor.

Denzil turned back, scarlet-faced. "I wasn't poking out my tongue, master," he said. "Honest. It just popped out all by itself."

"Lizards' tongues do that," said Valvasor, thoughtfully. "I would be very careful, if I were you. Maybe your hose are busting into holes because of the scales growing on your legs."

Alarmed, Denzil bent down and investigated his own knees. "Nothing there," he said, relieved.

Valvasor smiled, and his regal face creased into little lines of amusement and love. "I would like you, please, to deliver these bundles for me. Be very

9

careful with them, I don't want the leaves broken. Take the one with the red ribbon to Genevieve Grumpibones, the blue one to Sapphira Frowniface, and the green one to Kitty Wildbloode. Have you got that? Don't get them mixed up, whatever you do – you'll get me into the very worst kind of trouble."

"What are they?" asked Denzil, sniffing the bundles.

"Charms for St Valentine's Day," said Valvasor. "If a woman has five bay leaves scratched with the name of the man she wants to marry, then sleeps with four of the leaves under her bed and the fifth under her pillow, her wish will come true."

Denzil gave a scornful grunt. "Stupid love stuff," he said.

"It's very important to them," said Valvasor.

"Are you not going to speak spells over them?" asked Denzil. "They'll need a powerful lot of magic. A man would have to be blind to fall in love with Mother Frowniface!"

"That is unkind, Denzil. People cannot help the way they look. I'm not speaking spells over the leaves, because the magic lies in what the women themselves believe. Now go, deliver the leaves, and make sure each woman gets the right bundle. That is vital. Can you remember which bundle goes to which woman?"

Denzil nodded, forgetting the stolen raspberry pie in his pocket, and cramming the bundles on top of it. On the way out, he hesitated. "Master, are you definite about the ceremonial robe? Really absolutely no-changing-your-mind decided?"

Valvasor just frowned at him, and Denzil fled. As he trotted down the road he muttered colours and names to himself, "Green to Grumpibones, blue to Frownface, and red to Wildbloode. Or was it blue to Wildbloode? Oh, St Valentine help me! Green to Wildbloode. That was it! Blue to Grumpibones ... "

He came to Kitty Wildbloode's cottage, and stood outside her rickety fence, holding the three bundles. The bundles, smeared with raspberry jam, rustled in his shaking hands. At last he said a rhyme taught to him by Samantha, when she had helped him decide once which chocolate to choose. She called it a Choosing-Spell.

Eeny meeny miney mo,
Catch a piglet by the toe.
If it squeals let it go,
Eeny meeny miney mo.

Then he marched up to the cottage door, knocked loudly, dropped the bundle with the red ribbon on to her stone step, and fled. He delivered the blue bundle to Genevieve Grumpibones, and the green one to Sapphira Frownface. Then he hurried on to the fair, pleased with himself for thinking of Sam's spell.

He was tempted to send Sam something for St Valentine's Day, but thought she probably wouldn't know about St Valentine. She lived seven centuries into the future, and Denzil had gone to her place by accident once, when his spells had gone wrong. It had been a nice accident though, if a little worrying at

11

times. "She wouldn't know what a St Valentine's Day gift was for," he said aloud. "It's silly, anyway, all this stupid love stuff. I wouldn't mind if she sent me something, though – maybe a telephone, so we could talk, or a computer, so I could work out my spells easier. Or –" and he groaned with longing – "or the magic box they called TV, and the Star Wars galaxy. Oh, I wouldn't mind if she sent me that! I'd even kiss her, if she sent me *that*!"

As he passed Mother Gurtler's cobblestone courtyard, he noticed her ten little pigs warming themselves in the pale morning sun. The stones were golden in the light, but frost lay in the deep shadows along the wooden fences and around the small buildings sheltering hens and goats. The tiny shelters had thatched roofs, like Mother Gurtler's own cottage, and icicles dripped, glittering, in the late winter sun. Seeing the pigs, Denzil stopped, something important niggling on the edges of his mind.

"When pigs fly," Valvasor had said. Then the idea hit.

"That's when I can borrow his ceremonial robe!" Denzil shouted. "When pigs fly! He wasn't saying No at all! He was just answering me in a riddle!"

For a few moments he stood perfectly still, overwhelmed by the astounding brilliance of his revelation. Then he raced back to Valvasor's, flung open the door, and rushed in. The elderly wizard was still sorting out his dried herbs, and glanced up irritably.

"Home so soon?" he asked. "Was the fair dull?"

"Oh no, master!" cried Denzil, his face shining. "I haven't been there, yet. I realised what you meant. May I please use one of your books?"

"Very well, if it is for something important."

"Aye, it is," said Denzil. He got down the book with the shape-changing spells, and looked up the one he wanted.

For a brief while Valvasor studied him, puzzling over what it was this time that had made his apprentice so excited. Denzil often got suddenly excited, when a new idea hit him. He was hot-tempered, headstrong, and stubborn as a mule, but he was clever. The great wizard had known that from the day he first saw Denzil – from the day he found a grubby bundle left on his doorstep and unwrapped it to find a baby with black hair and extraordinary green eyes full of wisdom and fire. Valvasor was used to people leaving him the babies they could not afford to keep; he always found a good home for the children, where he knew they would be loved and safe. But this child – this strange, wild, other-worldly child – was gifted, and Valvasor had kept him and brought him up and trained him in the ways of magic. Denzil learned fast, and Valvasor was often astonished at the wonderful – and sometimes wicked – things he did. But he loved Denzil, and he smiled as he looked at him now, crouched over the book, a small cloud of white flour still floating about his hair.

Then Valvasor bent over his work again, and did not notice when Denzil slammed the book shut and raced outside. So lost was the great wizard in his sorting and selecting and labelling, that he did not notice the distant sounds of amazement and laughter; did not hear the children screaming, or the men shouting, or the squealing of frantic animals. But when the door was flung open and Denzil rushed over and grabbed his sleeve, shouting at him to come outside, Valvasor put down the dried plant he held, and noticed the clamour outside.

"What is it, lad?" he asked.

"They're flying!" cried Denzil, elated.

"What are?" asked Valvasor, suddenly suspicious.

"Go and look!" said Denzil, grinning, enormously pleased with himself. "Go on, master, go and look!"

Valvasor went to the door, stepped outside, and saw the most amazing sight.

Ten little pigs were flying above the thatched roof of Mother Gurtler's cottage, their round bottoms and curly tails bobbing gracefully in the breeze. The pigs had large pink wings, thin and smooth like bats' wings, that caught the updraughts of the wind and sent the squealing animals soaring over the chimney-holes.

"I had to make the wings big," said Denzil from behind the wizard. "The pigs were too fat and heavy, otherwise. And they fluttered around a bit at first, and couldn't rise above the ground. But once they got the idea, they were off."

Valvasor said nothing, he just looked at the frenzied pigs and all the people laughing at them. Several men were climbing ladders on to the cottage roof, long-handled nets in their hands. They swiped at the pigs as if they were butterflies, but the pigs wobbled off in opposite directions, squealing in terror.

Valvasor turned to the cottage interior, and looked at Denzil. The boy had his head in Valvasor's chest of clothes, and was tossing aside garments as if he were swimming through a kaleidoscope sea. At last he stood up, smiling, the wondrous ceremonial robe in his hands.

"Put that down," said Valvasor, his voice low with barely concealed fury.

Denzil stared at him, puzzled. "Why, master? I asked if I could have it and you said, 'When pigs fly'. So I made them fly. I thought it was a riddle, to see if I was clever enough –"

"I hope you're clever enough to undo that terrible spell," said Valvasor, still deadly quiet. "Go out now, lad, and undo the wrong. Put the pigs back where their home is, then come here and see me."

"I can't wear your robe to the fair, then?" asked Denzil, devastated.

"You'll not be going to the fair," said Valvasor. "You'll not be going anywhere for a very long time. Now go out and bring the pigs down, gently. Use a slow Undoing-Spell, and make sure each pig lands without injury."

Denzil swallowed nervously and went outside. The people saw him coming, and clapped and cheered. They complained when Denzil spoke the Undoing-Spell. When the pigs began to drift slowly down, the men tried to catch them with the nets, but Denzil

15

wouldn't let them. The village folk began to grumble, feeling cheated that their fun was over so soon. When all the pigs were back in Mother Gurtler's yard, wingless and grunting happily, Denzil went home.

Valvasor was sitting in his great carved chair, his face fierce and forbidding. He looked like a king, with his eyes blazing like blue fire, his mouth stern, and his beard flowing down his emerald green robe almost to his waist. He even sat like a king, straight and very still, his long, beautiful hands folded across his chest. Denzil stood in front of him, his head bent but his green eyes flashing defiantly.

"How old are you, Denzil?" asked Valvasor.

"Eleven, master. I think." Denzil started to count on his fingers, but Valvasor stopped him.

"You are old enough, then, to be a responsible and trustworthy wizard," said Valvasor. "Old enough to remember and respect the Great Laws. Old enough to know the true value of the special gifts you possess, and to honour them. Do you really understand what magic is for, Denzil?"

"To do things with," said Denzil.

"What kinds of things?"

Denzil shrugged, and hitched up his hose. He stared straight into Valvasor's deep and glowing eyes, and said recklessly, "Anything I want. It's my power."

"It is not your power," said Valvasor. "It is the huge power from which the stuff of life itself is made: the power of atoms and molecules, breath and word, time and eternity. It is to be used in harmony with all living things, for their good and their peace. Until now you

16

have had a great deal of fun with magic, and there is nothing wrong with that. I believe you have never touched another human being with your magic, against their will."

"No, never," said Denzil earnestly. "I never do anything they don't want. I promised you that. It's one of the Great Laws."

"Well then," said Valvasor, "the same applies to animals. I know there was a time when you turned all our village creatures into stones, and I cannot think that they were happy about it. I know there was a good reason for that, lad, and I was not angry. But today you changed the form and purpose of pigs, for no other reason than to achieve your own selfish desire."

"The pigs enjoyed it!" said Denzil.

"Did they?" asked Valvasor. "Did they tell you that?"

"No. Shall I make a Speaking-Spell, and go back and ask them?"

"I hope you jest, lad. I hope never again to see you make jokes of animals, or use them for your own gain or amusement. I want you to think about these things, while you sweep all the old straw out of the stable, burn it outside, and put new straw in. Think about it again while you brush down our donkey, comb the knots out of her mane, and untangle her tail. Think about it yet again while you take a sack to the fields, pull up the last of the winter carrots, and place them all in the wooden chest in the stable, next to the water trough which you will empty, scrub clean, and fill with fresh river water. Then you and the donkey may go for an evening stroll – for it will be evening by then

– and she will nuzzle your hand and thank you for your great kindness to her."

"Master, the fair will be over by then!" wailed Denzil, distraught. "I'll have missed it!"

"I know, son," said Valvasor.

Denzil went outside, got the old straw broom, and started furiously sweeping hay out of the stable. Clouds of dust poured out of the stable door and hovered above the frosty ground outside. The donkey watched the sudden flurry of activity, her huge eyes soft and surprised.

Valvasor appeared in the stable doorway, just as Denzil sent another cloud of dirt and filthy straw flying out. The great wizard was covered with it.

"Sorry," muttered Denzil.

The dirt and straw vanished, and Valvasor smiled. "I'm going to visit Mother Wyse for the day," he said. "No doubt I shall bring back a honey and hedgehog pie for you – which you shall have earned."

The wizard left, and Denzil went on cleaning the stable, grumbling to himself. Even the promise of his favourite pie couldn't wipe out his rage at missing the fair. He loved fairs, with their excitement and bustle – loved the jugglers, musicians, gypsies telling people's fortunes, strong men lifting ladies with one hand, the Punch and Judy puppet shows, and the village players who dressed up and performed plays. He especially adored the food – the colourful stalls brimming with toffee apples, apple pies, candied fruits, and . . .

"I *won't* miss it!" shouted Denzil, throwing the broom on to the stable floor. Breathing heavily, he thought for a while, his eyes gleaming. Then, slowly, carefully, he muttered a spell he had often used.

> *I give you, broom, this task to do:*
> *To sweep this stable place all through;*
> *To make anew and spread fresh straw*
> *All over the cleaned stable's floor.*
> *And sack that hangs upon the nail,*
> *You fly yourself to yonder dale*
> *Where carrots underneath a spell*
> *Will leap into you, fill you well;*
> *Then fly you back, and fill the chest*
> *Against the wall that faces west.*
> *Stale water in the donkey's trough,*
> *Time to flow up, out, and off!*
> *And waters fresh and clean and sweet,*
> *Time to give this beast a treat.*
> *And I command you, bristle-brush,*
> *To clean and rub and carefully wash*
> *This patient beast until she gleams.*
> *And this is last of all my schemes:*
> *That donkey, you will exercise*
> *Out in the fields, until the skies*
> *Grow dim, and then you will come back*
> *All safe and sound, and have a snack*
> *Of new-got carrots and fresh hay*
> *That I have not put here today.*

Then he hitched up his hose, got his warm woollen cloak from inside the house, and went whistling to the fair.

2 The Dancing Bear

e was only a short way from Valvasor's house, when another brilliant idea occurred to him: he could magic himself up a wondrous ceremonial robe! It wouldn't be a real one like Valvasor's, nor would it have the special powers that were woven into his; but it would be grand, and the village folk would admire him mightily. So, as he walked along, he imagined what his robe would look like. And, as he imagined, he got more and more excited, more carried away with his own brilliance. His robe would be better than Valvasor's – better than anything ever worn in the village, better than anything ever seen in the whole land! Sweating with excitement, and screwing up his face with the effort of concentration, Denzil gradually made a clear picture in his mind. Then, summoning the best magic he knew, he began to work his spell.

Slowly, like wet paint running down a grey page, amazing colours began spreading through his dull old clothes. Blues as deep as midnight skies flowed down his tunic, and rainbows streamed from his sleeves. Rough wool began to shine, became the finest silk; then he was all in blue, brilliant blue from his neck to his shoes. Scattered through his gown were silver stars and yellow harvest moons. The hem was pure gold and shining as the sun. He wore a cape the colours of the sunrise, and it swirled about him like clouds of fire, and in the glimmering folds flew dragons. The points of his satin shoes tinkled with silver bells as he walked. But most wonderful of all was his hat. Black as raven's wings, it was adorned with all the glories of the universe – with galaxies of stars, and phosphorescent lights, and floating silver orbs like moons. Dark mists, shot through with meteors, whirled about his hat, and twenty planets whizzed around his head. And so, almost lost within the whirling, swirling splendour of his creation, Denzil arrived at last at the fair.

What a commotion he caused! As he wandered among the village folk, with all his moons and stars spinning round and round, the people could hardly contain their astonishment. Children shrieked with excitement and tried to catch the spinning globes; men stared, puzzled, and tried to guess what wondrous machinery made it all work; and old people twittered and clucked, and said the hat was a hazard – which it was, because several people got too close, and were hit over the head by orbiting moons. An old man fainted and fell across a table of custard tarts, and Mother Gurtler got such a shock when she saw Denzil, she dropped the cage of chickens she had come to sell, and it broke, sending panic-stricken birds everywhere. Girls squealed and giggled, and ignored the young men who were trying to impress them; and the young men got jealous, said the wizard's costume was silly anyway, and went off to catch Mother Gurtler's frenzied fowls. Travelling players forgot their lines when they caught sight of Denzil, and jugglers dropped their balls. A knife-thrower missed his target altogether, and hit a nearby barrel of ale, slicing a hole in the wood, and letting all the ale out. That upset quite a few people. The miller, who was rather drunk by this time, took the knife-thrower's knives off him and threw them in the pond. Then the knife-thrower threw the miller in the pond, and they got into a fight.

Pretending not to notice the fuss, Denzil smiled and bowed politely to everyone. The moons spun wildly about his head and made the girls squeal again. Very pleased with his success, he wandered among the food stalls and sniffed at the marvellous medley of smells. Licking a huge red toffee apple, he lingered near the Punch and Judy show, but soon became bored with Punch belting Judy over the head. He thought of Sam and grinned to himself, thinking she'd flatten anyone who hit *her* over the head. Sam wasn't like the other girls he knew; she was bossy and bold, even fierce sometimes. She was the one person in the whole world, apart from Valvasor, who wasn't afraid of Denzil's magic. She could even do a bit of magic herself now, which Denzil found worrying. Sam had come to Denzil's village in the dead of last winter and Mother Wyse, herself a cunning worker in magic, had taught Sam a few spells.

Looking for something new to see, and still chomping on his toffee apple, Denzil stopped to watch an old gypsy woman reading girls their fortunes. The gypsy gazed deep into a crystal ball, and saw the names of the men the girls were going to marry. The girls were giggling, thrilled. This being St Valentine's Day, they were all thinking of love. Denzil pulled a face, and turned to watch a juggler instead.

He juggled wonderfully for a while, seven coloured balls going around like a rainbow about his head. Then he noticed Denzil and dropped a ball, and the rainbow plopped into the dust at his feet. The crowd watching scoffed at the juggler, and someone threw a rotten egg at him. Disappointed, Denzil turned away. The fair didn't seem so wonderful any more. He suddenly saw it as Sam might see it: clever but dusty people doing their best to make other people laugh. He'd seen far greater things when he'd visited Sam's world. There he'd seen an inspiring thing called a television, and watched what they called a video about shining knights fighting with swords of light in the place called the galaxy. There, at Sam's, he'd been taken in a roaring red monster called Kar, so fast that even the fastest horse would be slow beside it. And there'd been the motorbike. Oh, that motorbike...

Denzil sighed, thinking that he'd give anything for a ride on a motorbike again. He walked slowly, chewing the last of his apple, and didn't notice when people pointed at him and called out. Feeling lonely and unsatisfied, he wandered around searching for something even remotely exciting.

Then he saw the bear.

It was a young bear, brown and huge-pawed, with a gleaming black snout and round fluffy ears. It had ropes tied about its neck, and three men were dragging it over to a platform made of iron, that lay flat on the ground. People stood all around, wondering what the bear would do. The animal pulled back as it neared the square of iron, and the men hauled at it until it choked and skidded on its bottom with all its paws pushed out in front, trying desperately to stop itself. The people roared with laughter, and Denzil smiled too. The bear did look funny, like a naughty child being dragged to have a sore tooth pulled.

Denzil ran over to the gathering crowd, and got a good position at the front, only a few steps from the bear. It was grunting and snorting, and trying to cling with all its might to the dust skidding beneath it. But the men were strong; they got it at last on to the iron platform, and the bear did an amazing thing. It rose up on its hind paws and danced!

It was wonderful! It waved its front paws and hopped about, swaying and grunting. One of the men pulled a little flute from his pocket, and played a jaunty tune. The crowd, much bigger by now, roared its approval, and clapped. The bear lowered its front paws to the grass outside the platform, and tried to do a head-stand. The people laughed and clapped again, and the men wrenched on the ropes about the bear's neck, and got him back on to the platform to dance.

Denzil watched, enthralled. In all his world, he'd never seen anything as wonderful as that dancing bear. Though it was small, when it stood on its hind legs its head was level with Denzil's. It looked straight at him, and he wanted to put his arms around it and hug it. He loved everything about it; its beady black eyes, its round ears, its big paws waving in time to the music, its soft dark fur. Its mouth hung open as if it laughed with the people, and its tongue poked out, bright pink against the coal-black nose. The people laughed, delighted, yelling for more. But the bear fell down suddenly, and the man stopped playing the flute. He and one of his friends dragged the bear back to the tent. It limped as it trotted between them, and stumbled sometimes as if it were drunk. Everyone laughed and clapped and threw copper coins into the hat the third man passed around.

Alone now, Denzil stared after the bear as it vanished into the shadows of the tent. Then the two men came out again, slid ropes under the iron platform, and carried it carefully into the tent. As they passed him, Denzil said, "How did you teach him to dance?"

One of the men grinned. "Trick of the trade, lad," he said. His grin widened, and he added, "Not such a clever trick as that hat you're wearing, though. Where did you get it?"

"I made it myself," said Denzil, proudly puffing out his chest.

"You want to sell it?" asked the man, thinking he

could charge extra money from spectators, if he wore something that grand.

"Not for sale," said Denzil.

"A pity. Could be worth a fortune." The men went inside with their friend who had gathered up the money, and closed the tent flap.

Denzil stayed there, unwilling to leave. His heart still pounded with adoration and wonder for the bear: he *had* to see it again, and find out how they trained it. He glanced around the fair. For once, no one was watching him. The people were crowding about a muscular young man who was challenging someone to wrestle him. He claimed he had never been beaten, and there was a bag of gold for the person who could. The butcher's son, a skinny, reckless lad, was stripping off his shirt, and people were shouting encouragement.

While no one watched, Denzil stood very still and murmured a shape-changing spell. His awesome costume seemed to shrivel about him. Midnight blue, silver and gold became dull grey; and shining moons dwindled to vanishing point, became specks of light in bright black eyes. His face became hairy, his nose long and whiskery; and his body, covered in grey hair, shrank, plunging downwards to the ground. His hands and feet contracted into tiny paws, sharp-clawed and delicate; and behind him, curved and smooth and softest pink, was a magnificent long tail. At least, it was magnificent for a mouse. Denzil was rather fond of his tail when he was a mouse. Lifting it high above the yellow dust, he scuttled under the

26

edge of the tent, and stood quivering in the dark shadows just inside. The bear was in a cage with iron bars, and the men were going out of the tent.

Denzil crept further in. When the men had gone, he thought another spell. Within seconds the mouse grew, seemed to unfold like a fantastic flower, midnight-blue and silver and gold – and was Denzil again. He went over to the bear and tried to stroke it, poking his fingers through the cage. The bear shrank back, grunting and softly growling. It sat like a human child, its legs straight out in front of it. The ropes were still tied about the bear's neck, ready for the next time the men took it out to dance. The bear began licking one of its front paws, and Denzil noticed blood on the leathery pads.

"Are you hurt?" Denzil asked, peering more closely at the animal. It watched him out of frightened eyes. Every time Denzil moved, the bear cringed back against the iron bars. Denzil shrugged, disappointed.

"I thought you bears were big, brave animals," he said. "You're what Sam calls a wimp. That's what I'll call you. Wimpy."

He turned away, and examined the rest of the tent. There was nothing much in it, but a bit of straw scattered about, and a sack containing half-rotten meat, which Denzil supposed was Wimpy's supper. Then he noticed the metal plate that Wimpy danced upon, and went over to it.

"I'll show you how to dance, Wimpy!" he cried, jumping on to the plate, his moons bobbing madly about his head. The next instant he leapt off, howling and hopping in agony. He tore off his smoking shoes and threw them across the tent. Shocked, he bent over and examined the metal plate. He pulled one of the ropes, and the plate moved a little, then tilted. He realised it was suspended over a pit dug into the ground. The pit was full of red-hot coals.

Feeling sick with shock, the soles of his feet still smarting, he limped back to the bear. He crouched down and looked at the bear's hind paws. With horror, he saw that they were blistered and bleeding, the burned skin pink against the black fur all around. The bear continued licking its wounded front paws, grunting quietly.

Denzil stood up straight, his green eyes blazing with rage. He could hardly believe that the bear's dance, so funny for people to watch, was only Wimpy's desperate attempt to keep his feet off the scalding metal plate. Denzil was so angry he gripped the iron bars of the cage and shook them, but that only terrified the bear, and achieved nothing.

"I'm not leaving you here, Wimpy," Denzil said, in tears. "They're not going to make you do that again. Never, never again!"

But how could he stop them? Make their metal plate disappear? They'd get another one. Put out the fire? They'd light it again. Then Denzil's eyes rested on the bolt on the cage door. Slowly, he drew the bolt back, and opened the door. He opened it wide, thinking that Wimpy would race out, out to the fields and the vast world and freedom. But Wimpy crouched there, whimpering.

"Come on!" said Denzil, taking the ropes about the bear's neck, and pulling. Wimpy did not move, except to make a half-hearted attempt to bite through the ropes.

"I know," said Denzil, gently. "You think I'm going to make you dance again, don't you? But I won't. I wouldn't hurt you for anything in the world – not for a bag full of gold. Come on – run away from here! Now! Quick – before the men come back!"

But Wimpy cowered against the bars, snapping his teeth in a hopeless attempt to defend himself.

Denzil stood thinking, biting his nails. The bear was almost bigger than he was, so he knew it was useless trying to force him to go anywhere. He glanced nervously at the tent entrance. Then he made a big decision – one he was sure Valvasor would sternly disapprove of.

"I'm sorry, Wimpy," he muttered. "But I've got to. I've just absolutely, definitely got to. I'm sorry."

Quickly, because he knew it well and also knew he didn't have much time, he chanted:

Molecules and particles,
Elements and principles,
Fire and air, flesh and hair,
Water, earth, and grizzly bear,
Fractionise, reorganise,
Be reformed, and realise
You are suspended in my power,
Like this for one enchanted hour.

There was a whirling wind, a swirling and

churning in the air. The bear howled and pressed back further into its cage. A dark mist enveloped it, and its howls grew fainter and fainter, then died away. On the floor of the cage, shining against the coiled ropes in the filthy straw, lay a small stone image of a bear. Denzil picked it up, raced out of the tent, and fled for home.

3 The Most Terrible Kind of Trouble

ll the way, while he hobbled on the cold stones with his burned bare feet, Denzil tried frantically to think of an explanation for Valvasor. The wizard would know Denzil had not simply walked out of the fairground with the bear trotting happily along behind. He'd find out about the spell, for sure. And what if the bear's owners came looking for him? If they found Wimpy again, what would they do? For sure, they'd take the bear back and be more cruel to him than ever. And Denzil – well, he'd probably end up in prison. Burglaring bears was probably just as bad as burglaring pies or gold or other precious things. And some people even chopped thieves' hands off, so they could never steal again.

Denzil groaned and hid his hands in the misty rainbows on his sleeves. The bear-stone jiggled around inside his robe, feeling warm and vital, but it couldn't comfort Denzil, or calm his thumping heart. He cheered himself up with the thought that Valvasor would still be with Mother Wyse, exchanging spells and potions. "I'll have plenty of time," panted Denzil, as he trotted along. "I'll settle Wimpy down in the stable, then think up a fantastic explanation that'll impress Valvasor so much he'll actually congratulate me. 'I'm so proud of you, Denzil my son,' he'll say, 'you're a genius. A perpitrat... perpetratual... perpendicular... perpet... an unending wonder to me.' He could call me a few other things, too. Like marvellous and excellent and stupendous. He'll be so impressed! I've just got to think up a really good story. But that's all right. I've got all afternoon to figure something out."

But, to Denzil's horror, when he flung open the door of his home and raced in, Valvasor was already there. He was sitting in his huge carved chair, looking extremely grim.

"Where have you been?" demanded Valvasor. "You were supposed to clean out the stable and take the donkey for some exercise."

"I did all that," said Denzil, his face going scarlet.

"You were remarkably quick about it," said Valvasor. "I came home early, because Mother Wyse was busy. The broom was in a frenzy all on its own, and carrots were flying through the air like cannonballs."

Denzil gulped. "Perhaps I'd better explain, master," he said.

"While you're about it," said Valvasor, "you might like to explain that cosmic carnival you're wearing, and that ridiculous hat. They're hardly the sort of

32

thing to clean the stable in."

Denzil grabbed the hat off his head, and the moons swung out of control and one hit Valvasor on the nose.

"Sorry, master," mumbled Denzil, miserably. He thought of the bear-stone down the front of his robe, and guilt washed over him.

"I'm waiting," said Valvasor.

"I really wanted to go to the fair," said Denzil, hanging his head, and almost whispering. "I really, *really* wanted to go. And I wanted to wear something special."

"I know that," said Valvasor. "And I really, *really* wanted you to learn to take full responsibility for your actions, and to learn that animals, like people, are not to have our magic forced on them. But you don't learn, do you? You're a worry to me, Denzil. A perpetual worry. Before I was even gone, you laid your magic on an animal again!"

Denzil looked up, scarlet with guilt. "You *know*?" he gasped.

"Of course I know!" said Valvasor. "I saw it myself! The donkey was out in the fields galloping around, unable to stop – exercising itself, I presume, since you were too busy at the fair, to do it. At first I thought the poor animal was demented. Then I realised it was under a spell, and broke it. I've never seen the poor beast in such a lather, covered with sweat, and trembling so much it could hardly walk back to the stable. I am disappointed in you, Denzil. Disappointed, and angry, and sad. If you put one more spell on a helpless beast, I shall terminate our partnership. I do not wish to have an apprentice who persists in being disobedient and rebellious. Do you understand?"

"Yes, master," mumbled Denzil.

"I sincerely hope so, lad. Now, I want you to go and cover our donkey with a blanket for the night, and make sure she's comfortable. Then you can go straight to bed. There will be no supper for you tonight. But by the look of your face, and the mess all down your galaxy, you've eaten enough toffee-apples to fill your stomach for several days."

In tears, Denzil fled to the stable. He put a blanket over the donkey, patted her nose and whispered loving words to her, then sat down on the straw and took out the bear-stone. It was feeling very warm, and Denzil realised, with a shock, that the magic hour was almost over.

In a panic, he did the only thing he could do – he spoke another spell, to keep the bear in stone until tomorrow. Feeling empty and cold inside, he then chanted an Undoing Spell, and turned his wonderful midnight-blue garments back into the grimy, hole-ridden clothes they really were. Then, crushed by guilt and the grief that Valvasor might throw him out, he lay down on the stable floor, rested his head in his arms, and cried himself to sleep.

An hour or so later Valvasor crept into the stable and saw Denzil asleep in the straw. The wizard went back to the house, returning with several fur rugs and a small cushion. So gently that Denzil did not wake, he pressed the cushion beneath the boy's head, then tucked the furs snugly around him. Denzil gave a long, quivering sigh, and snored softly. Valvasor was about to go, when he noticed a stone bear in the straw beside Denzil's head. Mystified, the great wizard picked up the stone, turning it over and over in his hands. It was warm and pulsing, and Valvasor knew it was no ordinary stone.

"Oh, Denzil, son of my heart," he murmured, very quietly. "What else have you done?"

He put the bear back by Denzil's head, and stood quietly for a moment, thinking. Then he said, very softly, but with great authority:

> *Whatever spells in this place be,*
> *Whatever kind of wizardry:*
> *I cover them with greatest good,*
> *That all shall end just as it should.*

Then, knowing he had done all that in his great power he could do, Valvasor went inside to bed.

Valvasor was sitting at the table eating porridge when Denzil came inside, trailing the straw-covered furs and looking more like a scarecrow than ever. He got his old slippers from their place on the hearth and put them on, feeling guilty every time he felt the bear-stone move inside his shirt.

Without a word Valvasor got up and ladled porridge into a bowl for Denzil, and set it down at the opposite end of the table. Denzil sat behind it, looking bleary-eyed and troubled.

35

"Is there anything you would like to tell me, lad?" asked Valvasor, gently.

Denzil picked up his bone spoon and poked it absent-mindedly into the porridge. He shrugged. "Don't think so," he said.

"I just wondered," said Valvasor. "I thought perhaps you had seen something at the fair yesterday, that impressed you."

"Nothing much," said Denzil.

"Nothing?" repeated Valvasor, surprised. "No amazing tricks? No wild, exotic beasts? No snakes, or monkeys, or bears?"

Denzil's face went red, but he said nothing.

At that moment there were hurried footsteps outside, and there was a loud, fierce hammering on the door. Relieved, Denzil shot up to answer it.

Three women stood there, all red-faced and flustered, and mighty ferocious about something. They were Kitty Wildbloode, Sapphira Frowniface, and Genevieve Grumpibones.

"Is Valvasor in?" demanded Kitty Wildbloode.

Denzil nodded, and Kitty swept past him, striding inside with the other two close behind. Amazed, Denzil stared as Kitty Wildbloode marched up to Valvasor and shook something in his face. It was a small bundle tied with a red ribbon.

"Is *this*," she said furiously, "one of the charms you made yesterday, to win me my man on St Valentine's Day?"

Valvasor stood up. He looked bewildered and annoyed, for he was not used to village women bursting in on him like this. Normally he was treated with the greatest respect.

"Aye, my lady, it is," he said. "But that one with the red ribbon was for –"

"*It didn't work!*" shrieked Kitty Wildbloode, stamping her foot and throwing the bundle on the table. "I had a visit early this morning, from that stupid turkey that calls himself Sidney Surlylip. He came thundering on my door at the crack of dawn, swearing undying devotion, and begging me –"

"He is *not* a stupid turkey!" cried Genevieve Grumpibones, taking Kitty by the arm, and shaking her. "He's the handsomest man in the village! He's the sweetest, kindest – "

"He is *not* the handsomest!" shouted Sapphira Frowniface. "*My* man's the handsomest! But he's gone courting *you*, and I've got your old fool!"

They started arguing in earnest, fists flying. Valvasor gazed across the ruckus, and gave his apprentice one long look loaded with wrath. Then, in the blink of an eye, the great wizard vanished.

Denzil stood behind the women, suffering the awful suspicion that all this was his fault. He had got Valvasor into the most terrible kind of trouble, and himself into something even worse. This was going to be the end of his career in magic, for sure.

In a split second, he made a decision. He dived between the women's pounding feet and pitching petticoats, and found the head of the bear rug on the floor. He got a key from behind the bear's teeth, scrambled up, and rushed over to the wizard's

37

cupboard of precious things. He opened it, and took down the medallion that was the heart of all great spells to do with Time. Trembling, he slammed the cupboard shut, not bothering to lock it, and ran to the front door. But just as he was about to push it open, someone knocked loudly from the outside.

Denzil stretched up and peered through the tiny hole Valvasor had created in order to see who visitors were, before he opened the door. Because of what he often saw through that tiny hole, Valvasor had become very skilled at pretending he was not at home. And Denzil, peering through the hole now, was gripped by the same impulse. The visitor was one of the men from the fair, who owned Wimpy!

The man banged on the door again, and the door shook. "I know you're in there, wizard!" he yelled. "And I know you're guilty! You were seen running out of my tent. And you left your fancy shoes behind! My bear's missing. I want a word with you!"

Instantly, the three women were silent, staring at Denzil.

Denzil gave them a feeble grin, and shrugged his shoulders.

"What bear?" Sapphira Frowniface demanded. "Is Valvasor dealing in bears, now?"

"Only that one," said Denzil, pointing at the bear rug they were standing on. All three leapt aside.

The man outside hammered on the door again. "Open up!" he yelled, furiously. "I've got witnesses, you little thief!"

"Am not!" yelled Denzil. "I'm a burglar!"

"I'll see you hanged for this!" roared the man. "That bear was my livelihood!" He hammered again on the door, so ferociously that the three women screamed, and Denzil did the only useful thing he could think of at that moment – he disappeared.

Inside the stable, the donkey looked up, mildly shocked, as Denzil materialised inside the water-trough.

"Oh, saints preserve me!" Denzil whispered, frantically stepping out. He took off his soft leather slippers, rung the water out of them, and shot an embarrassed look at the snorting donkey. "No need to laugh!" Denzil hissed. "You don't always end up in the right place, either, when you're in a panic."

He took the bear-stone from its safe place down the front of his shirt. The stone was growing warmer by the moment, was already beginning to change. Denzil placed it carefully near his feet, within his shadow and therefore under his influence. As he stood up, he realised his clothes were covered in straw, with a fair sprinkling of mouse droppings; but that couldn't be helped. He smelled a bit, and should really have had his annual bath before he left, but that couldn't be helped, either. This was a dire emergency, and Sam would understand.

Shaking with fear and excitement, Denzil clutched the sacred medallion and spoke aloud a spell he had often thought about, just for fun, to amuse himself. Then, it had been only wishful thinking. But now it was in deadly earnest. Now he didn't only think the words, he said them. And in the speaking he released one of the greatest powers in the universe – the mighty creative power that changed form and fact, and crossed the barriers of time, and made impossible imaginings come true.

4 A Fugitive

am sat in her tree house and ate chocolate biscuits while she looked at her Valentine cards. She had seven – five from Floyd Fogarty, and two from people she didn't know. Floyd's were easy to recognise; he'd written *I love like Samantha MacAllister* with his special gold pen in red cardboard hearts. She'd seen him cutting out the hearts during maths. He'd cut carefully, his face screwed up with the effort, his tongue poking out like a juicy worm between his thick lips. He'd smiled at her while he'd made them, though she'd pretended not to notice.

Now she dropped his cards in the rubbish basket behind the door in her tree-house, and picked up one of the others. Sunlight slanted in through her tree-house window, glinting on her long fair curls and in her dancing blue eyes. She was pretty, with a mischievous grin and a warm sense of humour, but she could be fiercely tough at times. She adored animals, especially her rat, Murgatroyd, and her ginger cat, Joplin. Murgatroyd was sitting on her lap at that moment, gobbling up the biscuit crumbs she scattered down on his head. He was so tame now she hardly ever had to put him in his cage – so long as her cat Joplin wasn't about, of course! Joplin spent his whole life dreaming and scheming up wicked ways of wooing Murgatroyd into his jaws, but so far the rat had been too cunning.

A car pulled up in the drive below. It rattled to a stop, and Sam knew it was Adam, Theresa's boyfriend. Theresa was her sister, almost seventeen years old, tall and slender and attractive. The house door banged, and she heard Theresa's voice. Then she heard Adam give Theresa a Valentine's Day present, and a noisy kiss. There was a rustle of wrapping-paper, then a pause.

"What am I going to do with a book about fixing motors?" asked Theresa, sounding disappointed. "I haven't got a car!"

"But you're saving for one," said Adam.

"No I'm not. I've changed my mind. I'm saving to go to India."

"The book will still be useful. You'll know how to fix the motor on your rubber dinghy, when it breaks down on the way."

"I'm not going in a rubber dinghy!"

"You'll have to – you'll never save enough money for an air ticket."

"That's not funny, Adam."

"I wasn't trying to be funny. I'm trying to be helpful. Anyway, how was I to know you'd changed your mind? I thought you wanted to be one of those independent females who fixed her own car and didn't mind getting grease under her fingernails."

"I *am* independent!" she cried, furious. "And being independent means I can make my own decisions about my life, without asking for *your* permission."

"Pardon me for breathing! I'm sorry I didn't read your mind, but it's difficult when you keep changing it. I suppose this means you don't like your special present, then?"

"My *special* present? This is Valentine's Day! You're supposed to be romantic. Give me flowers, a dinner by candlelight, something beautiful. Not a book about fixing motors!"

"I'll be romantic, then," he said. "I'll take you out to dinner. We'll buy fish and chips and sit and eat them on that old seat under the trees by the cemetery."

"Very romantic, Adam!"

Sam giggled to herself, got another biscuit, and stroked Murgatroyd. Theresa and Adam were always arguing, these days. Sam hoped they wouldn't break up: she liked Adam, with his long untidy hair, beautiful tattoos, dark beard, leather clothes, and silver jewellery. Even Dad was used to Adam now, and didn't call him a gorilla any more. Besides, Adam had a university degree in physics, and was the only one who really understood how Denzil's magic worked. He understood things about time travel and shape-changing; he said it was all scientific, and used words like quantum theory, subatomic mathematics, and molecules being rearranged.

The argument below got louder and louder, and Sam peered out of her tree-house window. Theresa was shoving the book back into Adam's arms. "Go and exchange it for a dictionary!" Theresa shouted. "Find out what romantic means."

"I'll look up romantic, and you can look up words like appreciation and gratitude. I thought I'd bought you something really useful. How was I to know you'd changed your mind about a car, and decided to go to India instead? Sometimes I wish you'd be a bit more understanding."

"And *I* wish you were a bit more sensitive and caring and romantic!"

"I am!" said Adam. "I gave you my hanky in that movie the other night, when you were bawling your eyes out and smudging all your makeup. If it wasn't for me doing my caring thing, you'd have walked out of there looking like a grief-stricken panda. What do you want from me? Dying rosebuds and a big useless teddy bear?"

"I think a bear would be *lovely*!" said Theresa, and stormed inside. Adam threw the book into the car and followed her.

Sam finished the biscuits, popped Murgatroyd down the front of her shirt, and climbed down the tree-house ladder. When she went inside she found Adam and Theresa kissing in the kitchen. She pulled a face and went down to the lounge. Her mother was there, reading a book. While she read she twisted a short, fair curl around her finger; something she always did when she was worried. Sam turned the television on, and a car race exploded loudly on to the screen.

"Turn it down a bit, dear," said Mrs MacAllister.

44

"Gran's asleep. She hasn't had a good day; I took her to the doctor this morning. He said she must have peace and quiet."

"I wish she'd get better," said Sam, sitting down and dragging Murgatroyd out from between the buttons of her shirt. "She said she'd take me flying in a microlight."

"It might be a while before she can do that," said her mother. "She's got a bad heart, Sam. The slightest bit of excitement can make it go all wrong. She's got her pills to take when it does, but it's better if we can help her keep calm and peaceful. And that doesn't mean buzzing around in the sky in a metal mosquito."

"They're not metal," said Sam. "Adam said they're aluminium and plastic, with a lawn mower motor."

Mrs MacAllister looked shocked. "Then I sincerely hope she doesn't take you up in one. And for goodness' sake, Sam, put that rat back in its cage. If you lose it, you might never see it again. You know pets have been disappearing from this neighbourhood lately. So put him away, and on your way out, please shut the patio doors. That wind's got a bit cold."

With Murgatroyd clinging to the top of her fair head, Sam got up and crossed the room. She walked like a model, with poise and dignity, hoping all the time that Murgatroyd wouldn't do anything dastardly in her hair. As she moved to shut the sliding glass doors, a tremendous flash of light tore across the garden.

Bewildered, Sam stared up at the sky, thinking the brightness must have been lightening. But the skies were clear, except for a few fluffy summer clouds. Then she realised that the light was still there, shimmering like a bright mist across the flowers and trees. It seemed to gather in the centre of the lawn, where it swirled in strange patterns, sparkling and beautiful. And out of it, wearing the magic gold and silver medallion, and looking remarkably frantic even for him, came Denzil. He was not alone. Behind him, limping out of the misty light, and shaking its head in a bewildered way, was a grizzly bear.

"We've got visitors, Mum," said Sam.

"Oh dear, I really felt like a rest this afternoon," said Mrs MacAllister, combing her hair with her fingers. "Are you sure it's visitors? Not just someone collecting for Save the Children, or something?"

"I think he needs saving, himself," muttered Sam.

Denzil burst in, and threw himself into Mrs MacAllister's arms.

"He doesn't want me any more!" he wailed. "He's exterminated our partnership! And I didn't do anything! Honest! Just enchanted the donkey and the broom and a few carrots, and –"

"Oh, dear," murmured Mrs MacAllister, hugging him close and kissing the top of his head. She sniffed, noticed some straw and dirt in his tangled black hair, and stopped the kissing. But she still hugged him, and crooned soothingly while he sobbed out his woes.

Sam really admired her mother at that moment.

46

Mrs MacAllister was as cool and calm as could be, stroking Denzil's back and softly telling him that everything would be all right. It was as if she'd been sitting here all day just waiting for the arrival of a berserk wizard.

Theresa and Adam came in to see what all the noise was about.

"Denzil!" cried Adam, pleased, then realised that Denzil was distressed. He crouched on the floor by Mrs MacAllister, and put his arm about Denzil's shoulders.

"What is it, Denzil?" he asked, softly. "What's wrong?"

"Everything!" howled Denzil, letting go of Mrs MacAllister, and clinging instead to Adam. "I'm doomed! You should have seen the look Valvasor gave me, when the three spinsters went wild."

"Valvasor's got three wild women after him?" asked Adam, surprised.

"Yes! It was his magic, you see –"

"The crafty old coot!" said Adam, laughing. "I wish he'd tell *me* how he does it!"

"You're not funny," said Theresa, crossly. "You guys are all the same. You –"

She stopped, her gaze fixed on something in the garden outside. Her eyes bulged, and her mouth fell open.

"A bear!" she gasped. "There's a grizzly in our garden!"

"Don't be ridiculous, dear," said Mrs MacAllister, calmly. "We don't have grizzlies in this country."

"We do now," said Adam, standing up. Mrs MacAllister went white.

Denzil clung to Adam's sleeve. "You've got to save him!" Denzil cried. "They made him dance, and it was awful! They had these ropes around his neck, and they dragged him on to an iron plate, and everybody laughed because it looked funny, and it was horrible because nobody knew why, and the bear danced and its feet got burnt and they wouldn't let it stop, and I – I saved it."

"I think it'll be fun to have a bear," said Sam. "It's not very big, is it? We could take it for walks in the park, and feed it salmon, like they did on TV the other night."

"You're all being ridiculous," said Mrs MacAllister, standing up and risking a look out of the window. She sat down again, quickly, her hands trembling in her lap. "Denzil, you've got to take that thing back," she said, in her firmest don't-argue-with-me voice.

Denzil didn't know about not arguing.

"I can't!" he cried. "I told you! They made it dance, and I promised it I wouldn't let them do it again. It was awful, Mrs MacAllister!"

"I don't care how awful it was, Denzil," she said, speaking slowly and very calmly, though her voice shook. "That bear has to go back. And so do you, I'm afraid. We have Sam's grandmother staying with us, and there is simply no room for a wizard. I'm sorry, my dear. You'll just have to visit us another time."

"But I'm not visiting!" said Denzil. "I've come here to live. I told you, Valvasor's exterminated me."

"He didn't do a very thorough job," muttered Adam.

"He means terminated," said Mrs MacAllister. "Denzil's done something wrong, and Valvasor's terminated the apprenticeship."

"Do you mean you're not a wizard any more?" asked Sam, shocked.

"'Course I am," said Denzil, puffing out his chest. "I'll always be a wizard. Only I won't be learning from *him*, that's all."

Just then there was a dreadful yowling, howling noise from the garden. They all turned to the window, just in time to see Joplin in mid-flight towards the bear, his legs stretched out as if all the brakes were on, his fur sticking up on end. He looked like a cartoon cat, leaping through the air and trying to stop half-way. Joplin had done what he always did when a strange animal was in his territory – attacked first, and asked questions afterwards. But this time the questions had arrived a bit sooner than he expected. The bear wasn't too sure about the situation, either. He turned and fled, crashing through the bushes into the neighbour's property.

"Now you've done it!" shouted Sam, at Denzil. "You've gone and upset Joplin!"

"Who cares about Joplin?" yelled Denzil. "What about Wimpy?" And he raced outside and dived through the bushes after the bear, with Adam only seconds behind him. There was an almighty splash, a scream from Denzil, and a swear-word or two from Adam.

Mrs MacAllister sat down and covered her face with her hands. "The fish pond," she said. "The bear's fallen into Mr Gump's pond. Oh, Sam. He nearly shot your father that time he fell in when he was drunk, and got lost on his way home. Lord knows what he'll do to a *bear*."

Just then there was another splash, and another. They could hear Denzil spluttering and choking, and trying to chant spells. Adam roared at him to shut up and be useful. And through it all were the strange, frightened yelps of the bear, who must have thought that the fair was by far the easier thing to survive.

Sam and Theresa rushed next door to help, and Mrs MacAllister got up and went to the phone.

But halfway through dialling her husband's number, she put the receiver down again. She stood rubbing her forehead. She could feel a headache coming on. She took a few deep, calm breaths, and tried to ignore the shrieks and screams from next door. Obviously old Mr Gump was out for the day, or he'd have called the police by now, and there'd be sirens wailing and police dogs swarming all over the property.

After a while there was silence, apart from a lot of puffing and choking. Mrs MacAllister returned to the lounge, and looked out through the patio doors at the back lawn. The bear stood there, looking pitifully thin with its wet fur plastered close, and entangled bits of water lily looking bright green against the dark. The humans, too, looked pitiful and subdued as they stood in muddy puddles, dripping. Denzil and Sam stood on either side of the bear, their hands on his neck. Theresa was wringing water out of her long blonde curls and complaining about ruining her new skirt. Adam was gently pushing the bear from behind, trying to make it move. The bear was swinging its head slowly from side to side, and making wretched little grunting sounds that pulled at Mrs MacAllister's heart.

She went outside, and noticed the devastation through the trampled bushes into the Gump property. She rubbed her forehead again. "Well, Denzil," she said, "there's only one thing left for you to do, now."

Denzil gulped, and his eyes brimmed. "Do I have to go back?" he asked.

"No. Not immediately. But you do have to have a bath."

"Just had one," said Denzil.

"Don't argue," she warned. "Don't even open your mouth. Just do it. And afterwards, Sam will give you some clean clothes to put on."

"Any clothes I can find?" asked Denzil, perking up, thinking of the splendid pink ballet tights he'd worn last time he was here.

"I don't care what you put on – so long as it's clean," Mrs MacAllister said.

To everyone's astonishment, Denzil went off towards the bathroom without another word.

"Go and help him, Adam," said Mrs MacAllister. All too well she remembered Denzil's last bath here, with its howling and hullabaloo. She added, "And be very firm, Adam. Smack his bottom, if you have to. I don't want the bathroom flooded, I don't want to hear any swearing, and I certainly don't want the neighbours phoning up to ask if someone's being tortured. And when he's clean, hide him in Sam's room. I don't want him making any more surprise appearances. And have a shower yourself, if you like, since you've been in the fish pond, too. Theresa will get you some of her brother's clothes to wear."

Adam nodded, and went inside after Denzil.

"Theresa and Sam, take that poor animal out to the garage, and dry him with the hairdryer," said Mrs MacAllister. "Then give him a bowl of water, a rug to sleep on, and some steak from the fridge. Make sure there's nothing in the garage he can hurt himself on. When you've finished, make sure the garage windows and doors are properly closed, come inside, and wash your hands carefully with disinfectant. And wipe the hairdryer with it, too. Then have a good shower, and wash your hair as well."

"Why?" asked Sam, putting her arm about the bear's neck. "He's not sick."

"He may be riddled with diseases we don't even know about," said her mother. "So do as I say, and don't forget anything. And when you see your father, don't mention a thing about the bear. Or Denzil. I'll tell him at the right time. He's got a few problems at the moment, as well as having to adjust to his new job, and the last thing he needs is trouble at home."

"Aren't you glad Denzil's here?" asked Sam. "I thought you liked him, Mum."

"I do," sighed Mrs MacAllister, smiling a little. "I'm

very fond of him. But I don't need him right now, that's all, with your grandmother here to get peace and quiet."

"She'll love him," said Sam, eagerly. "She loves waifs. Remember all those cats she used to have?"

"Denzil isn't a waif now," her mother reminded her. "And he's considerably more trouble than a cat. He's a runaway, a fugitive from medieval law. We'll have to keep him here until it's all sorted out, I suppose." She glanced at her watch. "Your father's going to be home, soon!" she cried. "Quick – get that bear out of the way. And remember – not a whisper about our visitors. I'll tell your father when the time's right."

5 A Wonderful Illusion

r MacAllister took a long sip of his home-brewed beer, pushed his wavy black hair out of his eyes, relaxed back in his armchair, and gave his wife a weary smile.

"What a day!" he said. "I don't think I can cope much longer with this work, love. It's too stressful. You've got no idea what it's like being with people who suddenly arrive with impossible problems, and expect you to be an expert in everything from medical mysteries to mummifying armadillos. I feel as if my head's been taken off, shaken up, crammed full of useless information, sucked dry, and rammed back on again."

"I do know the feeling, actually," she replied. "Better than you realise. But you're only working in the library, darling. Surely books can't be that difficult."

"It's not the books," he groaned, "it's what people want to find in them. Still – better not to worry you with all my problems. How was your day, love?"

"Ah . . . All right," she said.

"That's good. Mum's okay? She was sleeping when

I looked in on her just now."

"She's been asleep all afternoon, fortunately."

"Why? Did something go wrong?"

Mrs MacAllister took a deep breath. "I hope you don't mind, darling," she said, "but we've got a visitor. He'll be staying for a little while. One of Sam's friends."

"That's all right," he said, taking another mouthful of beer. "I always said I'd like an open home, everyone welcome. Who is it?"

"Denzil."

Mr MacAllister choked on his beer, and sent a mouthful spraying across the room. "*Him?*" he spluttered, wiping at his chin with his sleeve. "Oh, God help us."

"I hope He will," said Mrs MacAllister. "We'll need all the help we can get. Denzil didn't come alone."

"Who else did he bring? A crew of circus performers, or just another magician like himself?"

"Not *who*," she said. "It's an animal."

"Oh, that's all right," said Mr MacAllister, with a relieved smile. He had been an actor and had a strong, sometimes fierce face, but when he smiled he looked gentle and handsome. "Another rat or something, is it?" he said. "It can live in the cage with Murgatroyd."

"Not a rat," she said, slowly. "Something a bit bigger, I'm afraid."

"Well, what is it?" he asked. "You can tell me, I won't throw a fit. I've got used to Denzil and his surprises."

"It's a bear," she said.

"A koala? Been bothering the Australians, has he?"

"No. It's a grizzly."

Mr MacAllister said nothing, but the beer glass slipped from his hand and crashed on the floor. He didn't even notice. His face was a strange colour, mottled red and purple. Mrs MacAllister went over to him and put her hand on his arm.

"Are you all right, darling?" she asked anxiously. He didn't answer, and she went on, in low, soothing tones. "It's only a young grizzly, very quiet. Not much bigger than a large dog. It's been ill-treated, that's why Denzil rescued it and brought it here. We can't refuse to help him with it, darling. We're always telling the children how important it is to respect animals. Well, now's the time to put our preaching into practice." She went out to the kitchen and came back with a cloth to mop up his spilled beer. While she did that, Mr MacAllister's face slowly returned to its normal colour. He even began to look quite cheerful.

"I know!" he cried suddenly, with a laugh. "He's created an illusion, hasn't he? Denzil. He's hypnotised you into *thinking* there's a bear."

"It's a wonderful illusion, then," she said. "Come out into the garage and have a look at it."

"No way! He's not fooling me! I know all about optical illusions – saw them often enough, when I was with the theatre! Ha, ha! So he's improved a bit, has he, with all that magic he could do? Good on him. He'll go a long way, that boy. He could have a

56

promising career in magic, make a fortune if he got on to TV. I wonder why he came to see us again, though? It's not even school holidays yet. Where is he?"

"He's hiding in Sam's room."

"Why?"

"He thought you might kill him. Everyone else wants to. Valvasor's fired him. I can't imagine why; my imagination simply doesn't stretch that far. He stole the bear from a carnival, and the owner wants to hang him. And there are three women, apparently, who aren't very thrilled with him either. He hasn't got a home, darling. He's a fugitive. He needs our love and understanding. And so does the bear. It's suffered horribly. You know how animals were treated in medieval times; used in dreadful ways for entertainment. That's why Denzil rescued it."

"I thought we'd sorted out all that ridiculous medieval stuff," said Mr MacAllister slowly, as if keeping calm were a great strain. "We agreed it was all a hoax, and Denzil was just a very talented magician, probably a skilled hypnotist as well. You're not going to start on all that wizard rubbish again, are you? Because, quite honestly, at the moment I'm not in the mood."

"I don't feel in the mood for Denzil, either," said Mrs MacAllister, "but we can't pretend he's not here, or that if we ignore him he'll go away. I'm afraid we're stuck with him – and with his medieval nonsense, as you call it. And if he's created an illusion with this bear, it's a very good one. I think you should come and see it. You'll be impressed."

Mr MacAllister sighed and stood up. "I'll see Denzil first," he said.

On Sam's closed door was a large notice, written in bright red and placed at eye level. It said: "DO NOT DISTERB UNDER ANY CIRCUMSTANSIS."

Mr MacAllister knocked. "May I come in?" he called.

"Are you in a good mood?" called back Sam.

"I must be," he replied. "I know who's here, and I haven't had a fit, or exploded, or smashed down your door and throttled anyone. *Yet*," he added under his breath, and Mrs MacAllister prodded him in the ribs.

There was whispering from within, and the door opened. Mr MacAllister began to walk in, then stopped, his mouth hanging open.

For a few seconds he thought he was looking at a small but magnificent Chinese emperor. Denzil was wearing a crimson silk dress richly embroidered with pale pink blossoms and little white birds. His black hair was long and wet and carefully combed down, and he looked solemn and dignified. But the Chinese dress was not quite long enough, and his thin ankles showed a few inches below the hem. Then Mr MacAllister noticed the purple tights and the orange slippers with huge pink pompoms.

"Heavens – it is you after all, Denzil, under all that finery!" Mr MacAllister laughed, going over to Denzil and giving him a big hug. "It's good to see you again! I missed you, in a weird, insane kind of a way."

"Greetings, sire," said Denzil, beaming.

"Where did you get that dress, Denzil?" asked Mrs MacAllister, frowning.

"It was in your wardrobe, Mum," said Sam. "You said he could wear whatever he wanted. I got the dress out of your wardrobe, and Gran said he could borrow her slippers. The tights are the ones I wore in the school play, when I was the Sugarplum Fairy."

"I remember when you wore that dress, love," Mr MacAllister said, slipping his arm about his wife's waist. "You wore that the first time we ever went out together. Makes me feel quite nostalgic ."

"What are you wearing for a belt, Denzil?" asked Mrs MacAllister, peering at the white garment Denzil had wrapped carefully around his waist. "That's not what I think it is, is it?" Then she added, laughing, "They're not mine, I hope!"

"They're Theresa's," said Sam. "I told him not to put them on, but he wouldn't listen. He was going to wear her knickers, too, and Gran's pink satin petticoat, and –"

"You can't wear those around your waist, Denzil," said Mrs MacAllister. "They're women's underclothes."

"Nice little pouches for putting things in," said Denzil, plunging his fists into the round white cups of the strange garment, and looking pleased. "I can carry crab-apples in here, and custard tarts, and chestnuts, and – "

"That's not what they're meant for," said Mrs MacAllister. "I think you'd better take them off, Denzil."

Denzil stuck out his chin and said stubbornly, "You said I could wear whatever I found."

"I didn't mean Theresa's bras. Or my Chinese dress, for that matter. What's wrong with shorts and a t-shirt?"

"I like these," said Denzil. "They're like proper ceremonial robes."

"Let him have them, for now anyway," said Mr MacAllister. "Who's going to see him, apart from us? Talking of seeing things . . . I believe you've brought something with you, Denzil."

"A bear," said Denzil. "Do you want to come and meet him?"

Mr MacAllister grinned. "Sure do. I can hardly bear the suspense."

Sam groaned, and led the way out to the garage. On the way Mr MacAllister chuckled, and ruffled Denzil's wet hair. "I bet this is one of your best tricks ever!" he said. "You'll have to tell me how you do these things, later. Your illusions really are quite sensational."

Denzil smiled and puffed out his chest. "Well, I thought I was clever," he agreed, "but Valvasor doesn't think so at the moment. He thinks I'm a pertit . . . perpen . . . perpendicul . . . eternal worry to him."

"Perpetual worry, I think you mean," smiled Mrs MacAllister, "though goodness knows what makes him say a thing like that."

They came to the door at the back of the garage, and Mrs MacAllister cautiously pushed it open. She went in, Mr MacAllister still chortling beside her.

The bear was lying on a rug in the back of the garage, its nose across its paws. Its eyes were closed, and it panted as if it were ill. A piece of newspaper was spread out in front of it, with a tipped-up bowl that had obviously contained water, and an untouched piece of steak. Theresa and Adam were crouched beside the bear, looking worried.

Mr MacAllister's chortle turned to a choke. He said a word Mrs MacAllister usually got mad at him for, but this time she didn't say anything. She stood looking at the bear, biting her lip and frowning. "It's sick," she said. "We'll have to get the vet."

Mr MacAllister's legs buckled, and he sat down suddenly on the large tool box just inside the garage door. He wiped his hands over his eyes, and swallowed a few times. He looked ill. But he gave Denzil a rather feeble grin, and said: "Very clever, lad. Have you hypnotised us? Or is this some kind of a hologram? Virtual reality, without all the technical equipment? Come on, you can tell me. I'm familiar with optical illusions, but I've never seen anything quite like this. What is it?"

"It's a bear," said Denzil.

"Yes, but it's not real, is it? I reckon we're all hypnotised. It's very clever, Denzil, but I don't like this kind of thing being done to me against my will. Snap your fingers, or do whatever you have to do to get us out of it."

"I don't think it'll be that simple, Mr Mac," said Adam, leaning forward and stroking the bear's ears.

61

The animal seemed to know it didn't mean him harm, and it put up its muzzle and licked Adam's hand, sniffing the steak scent still on Adam's fingers.

Mr MacAllister bent down and poked the bear's side. "It *feels* real," he said. The bear growled softly, and Mr MacAllister poked it again. "This is very clever, Denzil. I really am very impressed. But it's time you got us out of it."

He was still prodding the bear, and it suddenly lunged around and snapped at him, catching his fingers in its jaws. Mr MacAllister yelled and dragged his hand free, and the bear growled again.

"Ouch! I've been bitten!" bellowed Mr MacAllister, staring in disbelief at his injured hand. His fingers were bruised, and a nail was crushed and bleeding.

"Keep your voice down!" Mrs MacAllister pleaded. "You're upsetting the bear."

"You think the *bear's* upset?" he cried, shaking his hand in agony, and splashing blood all over his shirt.

Mrs MacAllister knelt in front of him and inspected his hand. "It does look bad, darling," she murmured. "I think we should get that seen to. Maybe it should be x-rayed; you could have a crushed bone."

"I wonder why the bear bit you, Dad?" said Theresa, puzzled. "He doesn't bite us."

"You look like the man who owned him, who made him dance on the hot plate," said Denzil. "That's why he bit you."

"Thanks, Denzil. Your kind explanation is a great comfort to me," said Mr MacAllister, and Denzil beamed, pleased to have been of help.

"Mrs Mac's right," said Adam. "You'd better have an x-ray. You'll probably need a tetanus injection, too, if it's a while since you've had one. The bear's teeth are in need of attention, and a good clean. You could pick up any kind of bacteria from them – something we've never even heard of, in the twentieth century."

"Oh, I'm pleased I'll be infected with something exotic," said Mr MacAllister, going white, then red. "I might experience plague, or some other spectacular medieval ailment. My doctor will be fascinated."

"Don't be silly, darling," said his wife. "Get into the car, and I'll take you to the emergency medical clinic. Hold the bear, Adam, while I take the car out."

"You can't start the car in here," said Adam. "You'll scare the bear out of its wits. I'll take Mr Mac in my Merc."

He and Mr MacAllister went outside, and Adam opened the passenger door of his old Mercedes Benz. "I'm not going anywhere in this," said Mr MacAllister. "I bet it hasn't got a warrant of fitness."

"It has," said Adam.

"You fixed the brakes, then?"

"No. But the stereo's terrific," replied Adam, grinning.

Mr MacAllister backed away from the car, and at that moment old Mr Gump came rushing up, waving a bit of paper.

"There you are!" cried the old man. "I've been knocking on every door on your house. I want to see you. Your kids have messed up my fish pond. I could have you lot for trespassing. Do you realise – "

Mr MacAllister didn't wait to hear any more. He leapt into Adam's car, hurt his backside on a large book lying on the seat, and muttered while he waited for Adam to get in and start the motor. Adam turned the key, but nothing happened. Mr MacAllister groaned. He was in a lot of pain, and he didn't need Mr Gump yelling at him through the open window. He tried to wind up the window, couldn't because of his hurt hand, and turned on the stereo instead. Adam was right: it was terrific. The volume, especially, was phenomenal. Suddenly the Mercedes' motor roared into life, and the car lurched down the drive and out on to the road, leaving behind it the thunder of electric guitars and throbbing of drums, and a pungent scent of burning oil.

Mrs MacAllister emerged from the garage, closed the door carefully behind her, and confronted Mr Gump.

The visitor was an elderly man with a startled rim of white hair and a bristling white moustache. He frowned constantly, even when he wasn't angry, and his long, impressive eyebrows had the fascinating habit of fluttering up and down when he was excited. And right now he was extremely excited.

"*Someone* from this property," he growled, his eyebrows in a frenzy, "someone – an entire football team, by the looks of it – came pell-mell through the bushes into my place, pulling out plants all over my garden, and threw the whole lot into my fish pond. The water's full of grass and leaves, and there's so much dirt in there, you can't see the bottom. I don't know what I'll do if any of my goldfish die."

"You could try frying them for breakfast," said a voice from the back door of the house. An old woman came down the steps. She looked pale and she moved slowly, but there was something spirited about her shrewd black eyes. She came and stood in front of Mr Gump.

"So you're the grumpy old gander from next door," she said.

"Mum . . . " pleaded Mrs MacAllister. "Stay out of this, please."

"I've heard about you," went on Gran. "You never talk to anyone, except to gripe. How do you expect to make friends?"

"I don't need friends," said Mr Gump. "People are nothing but trouble."

At that moment Sam and Denzil came out of the garage. They too shut the door carefully. Sam came and stood beside her grandmother, slipping her arm about the old woman's waist. "I'm glad you're feeling better, Gran," she whispered. Then she met Mr Gump's ferocious gaze, and lifted her chin. "Sorry about your pond, Mr Gump," she said. "It was an accident."

"Your father's going to be sorrier than you are," said Mr Gump. He turned back to Sam's mother. "My pond will have to be totally emptied and cleaned. I've got a quote for doing that, from proper pool-cleaning people. And I want my plants replaced. One of them was a Japanese maple I bought last week for seventy dollars. The little dolphin statue has also been

65

damaged. It'll have to be replaced, too. I trust there won't be any difficulty having this account paid? I've written it all down here, so there won't be any misunderstandings."

He shoved a piece of paper under Mrs MacAllister's nose.

"Six hundred dollars?" she cried.

"It's all itemised," said Mr Gump.

"What's six hundred dollars?" asked Denzil.

"A huge bag of gold," replied Sam, and Mr Gump stared at Denzil. He noticed the long black hair that looked as if it had been cut with a blunt knife (which it had), the red silk Chinese dress, purple tights, and the orange slippers. Fortunately he didn't notice the bras.

"Who are you?" he growled. "Someone from *The Mikado*?"

"A wizard's apprentice, actually," said Denzil, puffing out his chest and hitching up the bras, which had slipped around his hips.

"This is one of Sam's friends, Denzil," said Mrs MacAllister, quickly. "He'll be staying with us for a while."

"Well, I hope that after this he manages to keep on your property," said Mr Gump. "If I catch him on mine, I'll take him straight to the police. I don't tolerate thieves who swim in my pond."

"I'm not a thief!" cried Denzil. "I'm a burglar! And I didn't swim in your stupid lake! I went in after the b - "

Sam kicked Denzil's shin, and he gave a howl of outrage and pain.

"That's hardly fair, Mr Gump," said Mrs MacAllister. "You have no right to come over here and start accusing my guest of being a thief! He fell in your pond, that's true, and we'll reimburse you for any damages he caused. But I will *not* stand here and listen to you accuse him falsely."

"All kids are thieves," said Mr Gump.

Denzil tried to remember the spell for turning himself into a vicious little dog with sharp teeth. But before he recalled it, the old man was strutting off back to his own house. "Don't forget the account," Mr Gump called back over his shoulder. "I want it settled before the end of next week."

Mrs MacAllister sighed and climbed the steps to the back door. Sam and her grandmother followed, Sam's arm still about her waist. "He's a horrible old grouch, Mum," said Sam. "Don't worry about him."

"I don't," said her mother, "but I do worry about this account. How could four people and a bear – I mean, a barely alive cat – create so much havoc in someone's garden?"

Sam shrugged, and Gran looked bewildered.

"Barely alive cat?" Gran repeated. "Has something happened to Joplin?"

"Yes. He nearly drowned in Grumpy's fish pond," said Sam, thinking quickly. "We got him out, but we made a bit of a mess."

"Oh. Poor Joplin," said Gran. "Still, at least he hasn't disappeared altogether." Then she looked behind her. "Where's your friend gone, Sam?"

They all turned around, but Denzil had vanished.

Moments later they heard a shout from Mr Gump, and the furious yapping of a little dog.

"Get away from me!" they heard, and a thrashing of bushes, as if the old man was trying to hurry through his garden. "Go on! Get away! Go home!"

There was a lot of low growling, then a yell. They heard the old man muttering, and then his front door slammed.

Half a minute later Denzil came around the corner of the driveway, looking pleased with himself. He pulled a face as if he'd eaten something disgusting. "He hadn't washed his socks for a while," he said.

Sam's grandmother looked shocked, and opened her mouth to ask something. But Sam said quickly, "Give you a game of cards, Gran!" and hurried the old woman indoors.

Mrs MacAllister followed, her arm about Denzil's shoulders. "You're wicked, Denzil," she said, but she was smiling.

6 Deeper Into Difficulty

"Just let me stay for a little while, and I promise I won't be any bother," said Denzil, scooping a handful of baked beans off his plate, and sucking them noisily into his mouth. A few beans escaped, and he followed them along his wrist and up his arm with his tongue, catching them just on the inside of his elbow. Sam watched, fascinated.

"It's not you, Denzil, that's the bother," said Mrs MacAllister. "Well . . . not unless you continue to eat like that. If you can't use a knife and fork, use a spoon. Just as well Gran's having dinner in bed; if she saw you doing that, she'd have a fit."

"What's a fit?" asked Denzil.

"What I'm going to have in a minute," said Mr MacAllister, "if you don't stop licking your arm. You're not a dog."

"I was before, when I bit Master Gump's ankles," said Denzil, holding the spoon in front of his face, and squinting at himself in it. "Gawd, my nose has got big!" he cried, alarmed. "Am I *still* a dog?"

"Don't be ridiculous!" said Mr MacAllister, irritably. He was eating his baked beans with a spoon, too. His left hand was thickly bandaged.

Adam sat beside him, reading the BEARS section of an encyclopaedia. He had gone home for dinner, then come back with the book so he could share all the helpful information.

"Grizzlies can grow to a height of two and a half metres," said Adam. "They're generally clumsy and good-natured, but kill if they become enraged. They don't often attack human beings, unless they're annoyed."

"This grizzly's annoying me already," muttered Mr MacAllister.

"I meant, if the bear's annoyed, not the humans," said Adam. "I don't think the bears care how the humans feel while they're eating them."

"That is not funny," said Mr MacAllister.

"Well, ours is a nice bear," Sam said. "He even licked my hand before, to thank me when I gave him the steak."

"And so he should have," said Mr MacAllister. "He should have stood up on his hind legs and bowed, and sung you a thank you song. That steak was *my* dinner! I'm not eating baked beans again, just so that bear can have steak. He can learn to eat cat food like Joplin, or go without."

Joplin was sitting by the fridge at that moment, waiting for someone to remember that he hadn't had dinner. He pricked up his ears as they spoke his name, but no one was looking at him. For some strange reason, he seemed to have been completely forgotten. Offended, Joplin stuck his tail in the air and stalked outside to see if there were any fat little dinners flying around the garden.

"The bear has to eat what's natural for him," said Mrs MacAllister. "He's been badly mistreated, and needs looking after."

"He needs a vet," said Adam, looking up from the encyclopaedia. "I checked the bear's feet. They're badly burned, that's why it can hardly walk. The footpads haven't any skin left on them, and are infected. The animal needs antibiotics, and proper treatment for burns. It's got lice, too, and ulcers from ropes or something that had been around its neck. It's got an infection in one eye."

"Denzil could cure him," said Sam, and Mr MacAllister snorted. Ignoring the snort, Sam went on, "You could, couldn't you, Denzil? You can change things, alter shapes. You could fix a burn."

"No I can't," said Denzil. "Warts. I can only fix warts. Magic isn't a healing art, not for big things, anyway."

Mr MacAllister opened his mouth to say something sarcastic, but Mrs MacAllister said, quickly, "We'll take Wimpy to the vet first thing tomorrow. It's Saturday, but I think our vet's open in the morning."

"That'll be an interesting exercise," said Mr MacAllister. "What'll you do? Poke the bear into Joplin's cat box, throw it in the back seat, and take it down to Mr Biddles? Don't you think he'll be just a little bit surprised when you march in there with a grizzly?"

At that moment the door opened, and Sam's older brother, Travis, came in. He had been working late at the petrol station, fixing the motor on his own car, and was hungry.

"Hi, everyone!" he greeted them cheerfully, on his way through to the bathroom to clean up. Slowly he came back, a huge smile on his face, and he went over to Denzil and hugged his shoulders. He had saved Denzil's life once, and loved the little wizard like a brother.

"Hey! I like your outfit!" Travis said, standing back and admiring him. "What brought you back here? Got your spells wrong again, did you?"

Smiling happily, pleased to see his hero again, Denzil replied, "No. Got everything right, this time."

"That's debatable," muttered Mr MacAllister.

"What happened to your hand, Dad?" asked Travis, noticing the bandage. "Get squashed in a library book?"

"I got bitten by a grizzly bear."

Chuckling, Travis went off to the bathroom. "Funny," he called back, over his shoulder, "just half an hour ago a customer said he saw one of those, ambling off down the road."

Still laughing to himself, Travis had a good wash, combed his hair, and went back to the kitchen. The place was deserted. Plates of half-eaten dinner were still on the table, and a pot of semolina pudding was boiling over on the stove. Puzzled, Travis removed it and switched off the element. Then he went outside.

"Where is everyone?" he called. He noticed that

72

Adam's car had gone, and that it had left tyre marks on the drive. "Didn't think it could go that fast," he muttered.

He went back inside and looked for some dinner for himself. There were a few baked beans left on the stove, so he made some toast and dished the beans on to it. He decided to eat in the lounge, while he watched the news on television. On the way he looked into Gran's room. She was lying on her back softly snoring, but she heard the door creak, and opened her eyes.

"Hello, Gran," Travis said. "Can I come in?"

"I guess so, if your legs still work," she replied.

He grinned and went and sat on the edge of her bed. "I know this is another silly question, Gran," he said, "but has everyone in this house suddenly gone mad?"

"It is a silly question, dear," she said, sitting up and putting on her glasses. "They've been mad for years. Have you only just noticed?"

"They've all disappeared. They've left dinner on the table, and stuff burning on the stove, and they've rushed off somewhere in Adam's car. It all happened while I was in the bathroom getting cleaned up for dinner. They didn't even wait for me, or say where they were going. Have I got BO, or something?"

Gran sniffed. "I can only smell petrol and oil, dear, and I quite like those. Reminds me of the days when I had my own little plane, before your dear old granddad left the planet. He never liked me messing around with oily things, and it was only after –"

73

"I know, Gran. Where do you think they've all gone?"

"I have no idea. They've been peculiar all afternoon. All this decade, actually, but this afternoon in particular. I think it's something to with that Chinese Emperor friend of Sam's."

Travis frowned while he ate his baked beans. He was eighteen now, tall and good-looking, like his father, with dark straight hair that flopped over his eyes.

"*You're* not mad, you know," observed Gran softly, as she watched him eat.

"Thanks, Gran," he smiled. "That's a great comfort, especially in this family."

"I'm so glad you haven't got your father's temperament," Gran went on, quietly. "He's so highly-strung, so impetuous. Always making a major drama out of nothing."

"That's why he was such a good actor, I suppose," said Travis. "I think he misses the theatre; he has nowhere to let off steam, now."

"His job at the library will settle him down," Gran said. She was thoughtful for a moment, then added quietly, "You do know, don't you, that he's having terrible problems with his eyesight? And he doesn't just need glasses – there's something very wrong with his eyes."

Travis nodded. "Mum told me. It's making him awfully grumpy these days."

At that moment there was a screech of tyres in the driveway, and voices yelling, and car doors

74

slamming.

"I hope you lot are going to help me pay for that ticket!" shouted Adam.

"Not likely!" yelled Mr MacAllister. "It's your fault you were speeding."

"You told me to!"

Then Sam screeched, "He's still here! He's been here all the time! He never escaped, at all!"

Gran sighed, and slipped back down the bed and closed her eyes. "Tell them I'm asleep, dear," she said, as Travis went out.

In the kitchen, pandemonium broke loose. When they saw Travis, everyone started shouting and screaming, until Mr MacAllister roared louder than everyone else, and told them to be quiet. Then he turned on Travis.

"What was the big idea, telling us the bear was loose?" he asked. He was so mad, the veins in his neck stood out.

"It was a joke, Dad!" said Travis, trying to laugh, and failing. "I was joking. Same as you were, when you said you'd been bitten by a grizzly. I do apologise. I didn't realise that you're the only person in this family allowed to tell jokes, now."

Mr MacAllister sat down at the table, and bent his head in his good hand. "I'm sorry, son," he said, more quietly. "I never meant to yell at you like that. You see –" He looked up, his face a mixture of bewilderment and seriousness, arranged into an apologetic grin – "you see, Travis, I wasn't joking. I really *was* bitten by a bear."

75

Travis looked astonished, then suddenly he smiled. "Very good, Dad," he said. "Wonderful acting." He looked around at them all, his shoulders shaking with laughter. "You're all wonderful. You really got me going. I thought someone must have had a heart attack, and been rushed off to hospital."

"It'll probably happen, before this little visit of Denzil's is over," said Mr MacAllister, sighing.

Realisation burst across Travis's face, and he knew why they were all so serious about a bear. "Denzil, you little villain!" he said, beginning to laugh again. "Will you show me where it is?"

So Denzil took him out to the garage. They found Wimpy shuffling around the garage, sniffing everything he came to. He had knocked over a large bag of potting mixture, and trampled it all over the garage floor. Garden tools that had been propped tidily in a corner had all been knocked down and scattered about, and three boxes of sprouting seeds, carefully nurtured ready for planting in the vegetable garden outside, were covered in large paw-prints, the precious seedlings flattened. Wimpy heard them come in, and trotted over to greet them. He seemed much better, though he still limped, and he seemed to have trouble keeping his balance. Sniffing and snuffing, he pressed his snout against Denzil's chest, sensing that here was the human who had saved him from misery. Denzil noticed that the bear's nose was covered with a creamy foam, and he smelled strongly of something vaguely familiar. Travis too sniffed, as he bent and fondled Wimpy's ears.

"What have you given him to eat, Denzil?" he asked, puzzled.

Denzil looked at the steak still lying on the piece of newspaper, and the upturned bowl that had contained water. "He hasn't eaten anything we gave him," he said.

Wimpy hiccoughed in a contented way, then lumbered off in a wobbly line to the far corner of the garage. Grunting happily, he began slurping up something that had been spilled all over the floor.

Denzil and Travis rushed over to him, and Travis gave a cry of dismay.

Wimpy had knocked over the large plastic container of Mr MacAllister's home brew, and the floor was awash with beer. Paddling in it, Wimpy lowered his head and continued lapping contentedly.

"Stop him! We've got to stop him!" Travis shouted, trying to pull Wimpy away. But Wimpy, who had got a taste for the brew by now, growled warningly, and Travis quickly let him go. "Stop him, Denzil!" he cried.

But Denzil just shrugged, and said reasonably, "Nay – let him drink, Travis. At least he's getting something."

"Getting drunk, that's what he's getting," muttered Travis, half laughing though he was angry. "All that good home brew, going into a bear. Whatever happens, Denzil, don't tell Dad."

"Are you sure you'd be in trouble, if you went home?" Mrs MacAllister asked Denzil, when he and Sam were helping her with the dishes, and Denzil had managed in five minutes to break two plates and a glass. Mr MacAllister was sitting at the table drinking coffee, and mentally adding up the cost of the crockery Denzil was demolishing.

"A mighty lot of trouble," said Denzil confidently, polishing a knife and admiring himself in the shining blade. "If Valvasor doesn't kill me, Kitty Wildbloode will, and if she doesn't, the man from the fair says he'll hang me. If I go back, I'm done for. Can't I stay here for a little while?"

"What do you call a little while?" asked Mr MacAllister.

"About ten years," replied Denzil, and Mr MacAllister spluttered into his coffee.

"You'll be lucky to last ten hours, at this rate," Mr MacAllister growled. "Do you know what you've cost me so far, Denzil? Forty dollars for the doctor to sew up my hand, fifteen dollars for the steak we didn't eat for dinner, thirty dollars for the dishes and glass you've just broken, and a hundred and twenty dollars for the speeding ticket Adam got chasing the bear down the road while it was still safe in our garage. That's without the vet's fee for the bear tomorrow, and all the food we've got to buy, and the buckets of flea powder."

"There's that six hundred dollars Master Gump wants, too," said Denzil cheerfully, proud to be the one to remember. He wondered why there was such an awful silence.

"*What* six hundred dollars?" asked Mr MacAllister.

At that moment Travis came in from the garage. He had been out there with Adam and Theresa, mopping up the spilt beer and trying to get Wimpy to eat some solid food. Wimpy had simply stretched out on top of Mr MacAllister's potting mixture, hiccoughed softly, and dozed off. But every now and again in his sleep he licked his burnt paws, and grunted as if in pain.

"We've got to take Wimpy to a vet," Travis said. "The skin on his paws is all burnt off, and it's got infected. He's obviously in pain."

"I'll call Mr Biddles," said Mrs MacAllister, and picked up the phone.

"Don't give your name," advised Mr MacAllister. "Be careful what you say."

Sam stood close to her mother while she phoned, and they all listened.

"Hello," Mrs MacAllister said. "Mr Biddles? I'm sorry this is outside surgery hours, but we've got a bit of an emergency here ... Pardon? My name? Mrs Mac ... ah, Wimpy. Mrs Macawimpy. Yes, that's right. We've got a bear here, with burnt paws ... No, not a hare. A bear. A grizzly. A small one ... What was that, Mr Biddles? ... A joke? No, this isn't a joke ... Pardon?" She listened for a while, then put down the receiver. "Mr Biddles just hung up," she said, sounding shocked and indignant. "He says he's got better things to do than take hoax calls."

Mr MacAllister got up. With his good hand he picked up the phone. He spent a long time squinting at the list of phone numbers stuck on the wall,

79

muttering to himself, until his wife dialled the correct number for him. Then he leaned against the wall, frowning, and cleared his throat. In a deep voice full of quiet authority and calm common sense, he said, "Good evening. Macawimpy here. I think you need to understand something. My wife is not in the habit of making hoax calls. We do have a bear here, and it's urgently in need of your help . . . No, I'm not calling from the zoo, and I'm being extremely serious. What was that? The Ministry of Agriculture and Fisheries? What do you mean? Of course they haven't sent an inspector . . . Papers? What papers? No, the thing just arrived . . . No, it's not in quarantine, it's in our garage . . . No, I wouldn't like to give you my address. Pardon . . . What are you talking about, getting the law involved? Look here, there's no need to get all high-and-mighty with me! Of course I know about importing foreign species. I haven't brought in a plane-load of plague-ridden bandicoots, you know, it's only a bleeding bear . . . What? Totally illegal? I'll tell you what's illegal. Leaving an animal to suffer just because it hasn't got a passport, that's what's illegal. You call yourself a vet, Mr Biddles? If you had the slightest bit of compassion for animals, you'd get down here with your antibiotics and –"

There was a loud click as the vet hung up.

Slowly, Mr MacAllister put down the phone, and looked at Denzil. "Well, you've landed us in it now, lad," he said. "No vet's going to come and touch that bear. You should have taken it to an immigration place, and had it put in quarantine. You should have got the necessary papers, filled in all the right forms, had the thing properly inspected and approved, and all that."

Denzil gulped. "Gawd help me," he said.

"I don't think God's going to help you, lad, not unless He's good at forging papers and fumigating illegal animals."

"There's no need to get irreverent," said Mrs MacAllister. "We'll just have to manage without a vet, until Denzil takes the bear back."

"Can't take it back," said Denzil, stubbornly. "Got nowhere to take it."

"You'll find somewhere," said Mr MacAllister. "You've got until Sunday night, Denzil. I'm not going to prison for secretly importing illegal animals, just because you took a fancy to a flea-bitten bear at a circus."

"Would the SPCA help?" asked Travis.

"No one will help, according to the vet," said Mr MacAllister. "That bear's illegal; anyone who helps us with it is aiding and abetting criminals. I think it's time you realised the seriousness of this situation, Denzil, and did some serious thinking. I also think it's time you gave me some straight answers. Where did you get the bear?"

"From a fair," said Denzil.

"He means carnival," explained Sam.

"I know what he means," said her father. "Where was this circus, Denzil?"

"In Sir Godric's field, just by the Great Wood," said Denzil.

Mr MacAllister decided to ignore that. "Very well," he said. "Who owned the circus?"

"I don't know."

"It must have a name."

"It was just a fair. You know, like all of them – with jugglers, and Punch and Judy, and gypsies telling people's fortunes, and toffee apples, and knife-throwers, and . . . and the dancing bear."

"How did you get here, from the circus?"

"Umm . . . can't say, really," said Denzil, looking vague. "Not without giving away things Valvasor told me never to tell."

"What things?"

"Things to do with flying."

"Did you come here by private plane? Is that what the problem is? Valvasor flew you here, and he hasn't got a proper pilot's license?"

Sam giggled, and Denzil nodded eagerly. "That's what it is, my lord," he said. "No proper pilot's thing."

"It seems that you came without quite a few legal papers you're supposed to have," said Mr MacAllister. "I think I'll talk to this Valvasor fellow. What's your phone number, lad?"

"My what?"

"He hasn't got a phone, at home," said Sam.

"What's his address, then? I'll go and see Valvasor."

"Address?" gulped Denzil.

"Yes. Where you live," said Mr MacAllister, beginning to lose patience. "We went through all this last time you were here, Denzil, and it doesn't amuse me any more now than it did then. I'm tired of all this secrecy over your father."

"He's not my father."

"Your guardian, then. Where does he live?"

"Northwood Village," said Denzil. "Please don't go and see him, my lord. Please! He's as furious as a trapped ferret, with me! He's exterminated me! If he finds out what I've done with the bear, he'll kill me as well!" He fell on the floor in front of Mr MacAllister, and grabbed his feet. "Please, please, kind lord!" he begged, terrified. "Please don't go and see him!" Suddenly he remembered something and stood up, his panic miraculously vanishing. He hitched up the bras, stuck out his chin, and said, with great coolness and calm, "I just remembered. You can't go and see Valvasor, nor anyone else at my village."

"Is that so?" said Mr MacAllister, his chin jutting out in exactly the same stubborn manner.

"It is so, my lord," said Denzil. Between his finger and thumb he lifted the magical gold and silver medallion that hung about his neck, leaned close to Mr MacAllister, and waved it triumphantly under his nose. "You haven't got *this*," said Denzil. "And without *this*, you can't go anywhere. You're stuck here with your funny manor-halls and silly knives and forks, and you'll never see a castle, or King Edward's soldiers with their swords and armour, or have Mother Wyse's honey and hedgehog pie. And I will. I can go anywhere, do anything."

"And why is that, lad?"

"Because," said Denzil, "this is the most precious

thing in the whole land. It's beyond price, Valvasor says. It's worth is infinite; it's the rarest of all treasures, of incalab . . . incalcula . . . incalculib . . . you can't calculate how valuable it is. With this, I can go anywhere I want to. I can visit kings in their castles, I can fly to where dragons are, I can cross the whole cosmos – "

"Where did you get it, Denzil?" murmured Mr MacAllister, his eyes glittering dangerously. "Where did you get this antique locket of incalculable worth?"

"I burglared it."

"You stole it, you mean?"

Denzil went red, hitched up the bras again, and had the awful feeling he'd made another little mistake.

7 The Fight

lowly, looking so grim that Denzil didn't dare stop him, Mr MacAllister lifted the medallion from around Denzil's neck, and took it over to the light hanging over the kitchen sink. He turned the medallion in the brightness, inspecting the clever carving on it, the sun on the gold side, and the moon on the side that was silver. By accident, because his eyesight was bad, he found a little catch, and pressed it. The two halves of the medallion flew open, and he discovered a lock of silvery hair curled inside. He did not know it, but the hair belonged to Noah, taken from him when he was a thousand years old. The medallion was a powerful magic talisman – the most powerful thing in the world to do with Time. Whoever held it, and spoke the correct words, could cross days and months and even centuries. Some people – and Valvasor was such a person – could cross Time without it; but Denzil was still only learning magic, and he needed that medallion if he was ever to get home.

Denzil watched Mr MacAllister, his face pale, sweat gathering in little beads across his upper lip.

"Please, my lord," he begged huskily, "please give it back. I'm done for, if I lose that."

"Yes, I remember it was vital to you last time you were here," Mr MacAllister said, snapping the locket closed. "But you've stolen it, lad. I will give it back – but not to you. I'll give it back to Valvasor. All you have to do is tell me where I can find him."

"You can't!" squeaked Denzil, frantic. "You can't find him!"

"Then I guess I'll just have to sell this, to cover the cost of your little visit. I should get quite a lot for it; it's real gold and silver, by the look of it."

"You'll be sorry, Dad," warned Sam. "Denzil can't go back, without that. He'll be here forever, if you keep it."

"That's a risk I'll have to take," said Mr MacAllister, slipping the medallion into his pocket. "Think about it, Denzil: arrange a meeting between me and Valvasor, or I keep the locket. I'm going to sort this business out, once and for all. If your father does own a circus, he should be fined for cruelty to animals – probably closed down, if that bear is typical of his menagerie."

"It's not Valvasor's bear!" cried Sam. "You've got it all wrong, Dad!"

"I've got nothing wrong," said Mr MacAllister. "Well, nothing much wrong, apart from an illegal grizzly in my garage, a runaway thief taking refuge under my roof, a whole family gone berserk, and a sick mother likely to have a major heart attack at the slightest bit of excitement. I think I can cope with all that."

"A few hours ago, you couldn't cope with your job at the library," Mrs MacAllister pointed out. "And have you really thought about the consequences of Denzil staying? For a start, he'll have to go to school. And we'll have to buy – "

"Oh, I'd love him to come to school!" cried Sam, overjoyed. "I can just imagine him in my class!"

"So can I," said Mr MacAllister, "and I have the feeling he'd be expelled after five minutes."

"He can't go to school with you, Sam, I'm sorry," said Travis. "We have to be very careful where Denzil goes, what he sees. If he takes a new idea back with him, he could alter history. Not necessarily for the better. We've got to keep his life simple, and as close as possible to what he's used to."

"And what would that be?" asked Mr MacAllister. "Life at a circus? I imagine we'd imitate a circus very well. We've got half the animals: a grizzly bear, a lunatic cat, a few clowns, a trained rat – I'm sure we could pick up an elephant somewhere, and –"

Suddenly Sam gave a loud wail. "Murgatroyd!" she cried, her face white. Then she raced off into the lounge, and they heard her pushing furniture around, and making funny little squeaking noises the way she always did when she was looking for her rat. A few moments later she rushed in again.

"I've lost him!" She wailed. "He must have jumped off my head when Denzil arrived! He's been gone for *hours*! He could be anywhere by now!"

"Probably in the pantry," said Mr MacAllister,

"gnawing his way through the muesli we were going to have for breakfast. Between him and that bear, we could die of starvation by the end of the week."

"I don't think there's much danger of that, dear," smiled his wife. She added, to Sam: "Don't worry about Murgatroyd, dear. He'll turn up. He always does. So long as he isn't in Theresa's room, it'll be all right."

"If he's in Theresa's room, we'll know soon enough," said Travis. "She'll make more fuss than Denzil makes having a bath."

"I don't make a fuss," said Denzil. "Not any more, now I know that my hair stays on and my skin doesn't fall off. Everything gets a bit wrinkled, that's all. Even funny little bits, like my – "

"Really Denzil," said Mrs MacAllister quickly, "I don't think anyone is interested in which of your funny little bits gets wrinkled in the bath."

"I'm interested," said Sam.

"No, you're not," said her father. "There's only one thing – "

"My fingers," said Denzil, wriggling them at Sam, and grinning. "My fingers get wrinkled."

Sam giggled, and Mr MacAllister went on, irritably, "What I was going to say, was that there's only one thing we're all interested in right now, and that's what Denzil is going to do to solve his problem."

"I have solved it," said Denzil. "I gave the bear to Sam."

"That's not solving the problem, Denzil," said

88

Travis, "it's just shifting it around. Are you sure you can't go back and talk to Valvasor?"

"No," said Denzil, shaking his head emphatically. "Definitely not."

"Then what *are* you going to do?" asked Mrs MacAllister.

Denzil thought for a few minutes. Finally he hooked his thumbs through the bra straps, stuck out his chin in a lordly manner, and stood very straight as if he were about to make an important announcement. "I have no idea," he said.

"You'd better get an idea very soon," said Mr MacAllister testily, "because I'm beginning to lose my patience. That bear's already cost me a heap of money. It'll get worse, if anyone finds out it's here. There's probably a heavy fine for illegally importing animals – possibly even a prison term. At the very least, you'd better start mowing lawns and earning money to feed the beast."

"What's mowing lawns?" asked Denzil.

Mr MacAllister stared at him closely, his dark, shrewd eyes narrowed. "Sometimes I worry about you, Denzil," he murmured. "What does that Valvasor person teach you?"

"Nothing, now," said Denzil, mournfully. "He's exterminated me."

"I must admit, I'm very tempted to do a bit of exterminating, myself," said Mr MacAllister.

"But I'll manage," said Denzil, brightening. "You'll see. I'll set myself up here in your village, and people can come to me for potions and charms, and I'll fix their warts and find their lost chickens, and make their hair grow again if they get bald, and – "

"I'm afraid it won't work, Denzil," said Mrs MacAllister. "In this day and age, there isn't much demand for that sort of thing."

"I think there is," said Travis. "He could run his own hair-restoration business. I reckon he'd make a fortune."

"Aye, I would!" cried Denzil, eagerly. "And people would come from miles around to see the bear, as well, just like they did for the fair, and I could make just as much gold from the bear as I can from growing people's hair. But I wouldn't make him dance, of course."

"You could call it the Hair & Bear Business," said Sam.

"See?" cried Denzil, turning to Mr MacAllister, his hands clasped pleadingly in front of him. "I could be really successful here, I promise! And all the gold I make will help pay for Wimpy's food."

Mr MacAllister went purple, and the joy faded from Denzil's face.

"I think the best thing you can do," said Mr MacAllister in a low voice that shook with anger, "is to phone Valvasor, or call a neighbour to give him an urgent message, and tell him to get around here right now. I'll give you an hour. One hour. Mrs MacAllister and I are going for an evening walk. When we get back, I want to see Valvasor sitting in this kitchen. Got that?"

Denzil gulped.

"Good," said Mr MacAllister, taking his wife's hand.

They went out, and Denzil wailed and collapsed in a chair. "Oh, Jesus, Gawd, Saint Peter, help me!" he howled. "Oh, ill-fated day! I'm doomed! I'm doomed!"

Just then Theresa and Adam came into the house. "You're not as ill-fated as that bear of yours," said Adam, with a grin. "He's going to have an awful hangover when he wakes up. I think you should stay out there with him, Denzil, and make sure he doesn't get into any more trouble."

Denzil rushed out to the garage. Sam was about to follow him, but Travis stopped her. "Give him a bit of time on his own, Sam," he said. "He needs to think. Maybe you'd better go and find Joplin and bring him inside, before it gets dark."

Sam went out into the garden, whistling for Joplin. He always came when she whistled, no matter how far away he was. But tonight she whistled for several minutes, and he did not come. She went all around the house whistling, but there was no familiar drumming of little paws on the ground as he bounded towards her, nor the soft, loving meow that usually answered her. Beginning to feel very uneasy, Sam went all around the house again, and through all the garden. Still no sign of Joplin. She saw Theresa and Adam sitting in the old Mercedes kissing, and she stuck her head in the open window and asked if they'd seen Joplin.

"No, we haven't," said Theresa crossly, drawing away from Adam, and smoothing down her tousled hair. "Get lost. We're busy."

"No you're not, you're smooching," said Sam. "Have you seen Joplin?"

Theresa sighed. "No. Not since he and Wimpy had that fight in Grumpy's swimming pool. Now get lost."

"I think I saw him in the kitchen while you were all having dinner," said Adam. "He won't be far away, Sam."

"But he won't come when I call him!" wailed Sam.

"Oh, for goodness' sake!" cried Theresa. "It's only a cat!"

"He's not just a cat," said Adam, getting out of the car. "He's Joplin. I'll help you look for him, Sam."

"Adam!" cried Theresa, furiously. "If you put that stupid cat ahead of time with me –"

Adam poked his head back into the car and said quietly, hoping Sam wouldn't hear, "People's animals are still going missing. Forty pets have disappeared in this neighbourhood in the past three weeks, and the police are advising people to keep their animals secure at night. If you've got any heart at all, you'll help us look for Joplin. Sam will be devastated if anything happens to him."

Theresa got out of the car and slammed the door. "Oh, I've got a heart, all right!" she said. "And it certainly doesn't belong to *you*! Since you're so worried about the neighbourhood livestock, *you* help Sam look for her wretched cat, and then you can go home. Don't bother saying goodnight."

Adam sighed heavily, and his eyes were sad as he watched Theresa flounce off into the house. "We'll find him, Sam," he said softly. "We'll look up and down the street. He may be sitting on the footpath, waiting for your mum and dad to come back."

But though they looked everywhere, and asked at the neighbouring houses, there was no sign of Joplin. Sam was almost in tears by the time she and Adam got home.

"He's probably sulking somewhere," said Adam, as he got into his car to leave. "I bet he's deliberately hiding, just to let you know how annoyed he is with that great hairy catastrophe in the garage."

Sam chewed her lip, and frowned. "We were talking about missing pets, in school," she said. "Floyd Foggarty's rabbits vanished, right out of their hutch. It wasn't a dog that got them, either, because the ground wasn't dug up, and the cage wasn't broken. They just disappeared. And Amanda O'Connor's dog has gone, too. She had to go home from school on Friday, she was crying so hard."

Adam said nothing, and Sam went on, "What's happening, Adam? Why are all the pets going missing?"

"I don't know. Why don't you go and see how Denzil and Wimpy are? Joplin might even be in the garage, keeping an eye on them. We didn't look in there, did we?"

"Okay. Thanks for helping."

"You're welcome," Adam smiled, and his earrings flashed in the reflections from the car lights, before he drove off down the driveway.

In the garage Sam found Denzil sitting on the floor,

his arms about the bear's neck. Wimpy was snoring, still hiccoughing occasionally, and making soft little contented bear noises. But every now and again he twitched in pain, and licked his paws.

Sam looked all around the garage for Joplin, didn't find him, and sat down by Denzil. "Joplin's lost," she said.

Denzil stroked the bear's snout, and murmured in a voice that shook: "I can't wake Wimpy up. You don't think he's dying, do you? The miller got mighty drunk once, and no one could rouse him for three days. Valvasor said he had poisoning from it, and had to give him some potions, else he would have been as dead as a door-knob."

"He's not dying, he's just drunk," said Sam, stroking Wimpy's back. His fur was wonderfully soft, and she could feel his side rising and falling as he breathed. She noticed the pads on his paws, and how the skin on them was raw and bleeding. And there were raw patches on his neck, from rope-burns. "Are you sure you can't cure him, Denzil?" she asked. "If you can cure a wart, surely a burn wouldn't be too difficult."

"I've watched Valvasor cure burns," said Denzil. "He uses oil of peppermint, and St John's wort oil for pain."

"*Wart* oil?" cried Sam, disgusted.

"Different wort. It's a herb."

Sam sighed. "I think we'd be better off with a vet," she said. "We have to get him to one, Denzil." Suddenly she gripped Denzil's arm, her face alight. "I know! You could turn Wimpy into a dog! Then we could take him to the vet, and afterwards he could live here with us, and you could go back to Valvasor!"

"I can't go back. The man from the fair will hang me for a thief. And Valvasor won't help; he's wild with me, wilder than a wild ferret. I'll never go back. Anyway, I can't now, even if I wanted to; your father has my Time charm. I can't go without that."

"But you could still put a spell on Wimpy, and turn him into a dog."

"Can't," said Denzil, shaking his head firmly. "Valvasor said I must never again put spells on animals."

"Is that what you did, to make him mad?"

"Yes. I put spells on Mother Gurtler's little pigs, to make them fly."

Sam giggled. "Did you? Wow! I bet they looked cute!"

"They did," grinned Denzil. "Valvasor wasn't impressed, though everyone else in the village was. I was quite a hero – until Valvasor found out."

"What did he do?"

"He said I mustn't put magic on anything without its permission. Anything alive, that is. He said it's time I was responsible, and didn't play with magic any more. And after he said that, I put a spell on Wimpy, so I could bring him home from the fair. I messed up some other spells, too, that Valvasor had done, and got him in trouble with the three spinsters. Big trouble. "

"But he wouldn't fire you, just for that," said Sam.

"Would he?"

"Oh, no!" cried Denzil, shocked. "He'd never set me on fire! He just exterminated me."

Sam smiled a little, and sighed.

A flea hopped along Denzil's purple tights, and he squashed it between his thumb nails. "Valvasor's got dried herb leaves, to get rid of fleas," he told her. "He keeps them in all our clothes, and in our furs on the floor. I like the smell of them." He sounded sad, and Sam put her arm about his shoulders. To her surprise, he didn't pull away.

"Valvasor would know how to help Wimpy, wouldn't he?" asked Sam, and Denzil gave a little nod and wiped his nose on his red silk sleeve.

"He's very skilled at curing animals," he said. "He can mend bones, and wounds, and all sorts of ailments. He's got a wondrous supply of potions and herbs. His poultices cure anything. They stink worse than a pig-pen in high summer, but they work."

"I think you should go back and talk to him, Denzil. It wouldn't take you long, with your magic. You can take me with you, if you want. I'll help you explain."

A small smile twitched at the corner of Denzil's mouth. "It would be safe this time," he said, "since you're not dressed like an angel."

They laughed together, remembering. Last Christmas Denzil had taken Sam to his world, and she had arrived in a burst of brilliant light, dressed as an angel for her school Christmas play. "Remember how everyone thought I was a *real* angel?" giggled

96

Sam. "And how they all came asking for miracles and wonders?"

"And I had to do magic, to give them all their miracles," chuckled Denzil. "I had to give Baldie some beautiful long hair, and make Mistress Smallbones as tall as her gigantic husband, and make all the village folks' warts disappear."

"And you made a whole lot of hens for Mother Gurtler," said Sam. "But you got a bit carried away, and there were hens all over the village! Everyone was having such a wonderful time, enjoying all the wonders you made."

"I'm not allowed to have fun with magic, any more," said Denzil, gloomily. "I've got to be responsible."

"I thought you *were* being responsible. Besides, Valvasor told you to give the people their miracles. He encouraged you."

"He doesn't now."

"He's not your boss now. You can do what you like. So why don't you turn Wimpy into a dog, so we can take him to the vet?"

"Just because Valvasor's not training me now, doesn't mean I can break the Great Laws," said Denzil. "I still want to be a good wizard."

"You *are* a good wizard! And who made the rules, anyway? If you want to put magic on a bear to save its life, you're allowed!"

"No I'm not! I want to do things properly, Sam! If I don't use magic the way it's meant to be used, it'll disappear. I'll lose my powers, if I'm wicked."

97

"You're not wicked if you try to help Wimpy. You turned Murgatroyd into stone once, to save his life, and that wasn't wicked. You change yourself into different things, and it's all right."

"That's because I *choose* to do it to myself! But changing something when it doesn't want to be changed – that's wicked. I can't do that."

"Not even to save something's life?"

"No."

Sam removed her arm from about his shoulders, and her face went hard and cold. "So you'll let Wimpy suffer," she said, "just because you're too scared to use your stupid magic? I guess it's no good asking you to help me find Joplin, either – you'll be too scared to use magic on him, as well."

Denzil jumped up, and his green eyes flashed dangerously. "I'm *not* scared!" he shouted.

"You are so!" cried Sam. "You're scared of Valvasor, and he isn't even here!"

"You don't know him! He can see everything – he can see through Time and Space, and he knows – he *knows* – if I do something wrong! He reads my mind!"

"Good! He might be reading it right now, so tell him to get over here and see my father!"

"Aye, I just might do that!"

"Go on, then!" she challenged. "Do it!"

Denzil stared at her, his face scarlet with rage. She noticed tiny yellow lights exploding all about him, and a red glow seemed to come from his skin.

"I hate you, Sammy Snarlybritches!" he hissed.

"And I hate you, you useless purple-legged

98

milksop!" spat Sam. "You're a coward. A chicken-livered wimp."

Denzil's eyes glowed strangely, and he muttered through clenched teeth:

Golden hair go gleamy green,
Skin and eyes turn –

"Turn your own hair green, you horrible little toad!" shouted Sam, and stormed off out of the garage. After a moment she stuck her head back in the doorway. "Anyway, you can't put a spell on me, you'll break your stupid rules! Then you'll lose your magic powers, and *really* be in trouble!"

Denzil stopped the spell. "I'm already in dire distress!" he snapped. "A bit more won't make much difference!"

"You know what your trouble is?" Sam cried. "You're selfish! All you're worried about is your own skin. Wimpy's suffering, and it's all your fault, and you won't help him! It's your fault that Joplin's missing, too! And Murgatroyd! If you hadn't come, everything would be all right! I hope Valvasor *does* read your mind, and drags you back to your own world! I hope he does exterminate you, good and proper! I hope the three spinsters tear you into little bits and feed you to a dragon! I wish you'd vanish, and I'd never see you again!"

Then, almost crying with rage, she ran into the house.

8 The Strange Angel

As she passed Gran's room, Sam heard the old lady call out. "Is that you, Sam? Would you come in here a moment, dear?"

Sam went in, and Gran said, "I was wondering whether you'd mind making me a cup of tea." Then she sat up in bed, and peered at Sam over her glasses. "You look upset, dear," Gran added, sympathetically. "Come and sit down, and tell me all about it."

Sam shut the door behind her, and sat down on the edge of the bed. She stared at her hands, and noticed that they were shaking. Then, to her dismay, she started to cry. She was furious with herself, but the more she tried to stop, the harder she cried.

Gran pulled Sam into her arms, and patted her back. "Tell your old grandmother all about it, sweetheart," she said, soothingly. "I'm sure nothing's happened that we can't work out. Is it because of your hair? I wouldn't worry too much. Those colours wash out after a few shampoos. Besides, I quite like that green. Is it for a school play?"

Sam howled louder. "It's not – not my – hair!" she

sobbed, her face buried in Gran's shoulder.

"Well, what is it, then?"

"It's Joplin. He's missing. And Murgatroyd," wailed Sam.

"Oh dear," murmured Gran.

"And there's Denzil," choked Sam.

"Denzil? The Chinese Emperor?" said Gran. "Is he missing, too?"

"He's not a Chinese Emperor. He's a wizard. And he's not missing. We had an awful fight."

"What was it about?" asked Gran.

"I can't tell you!" choked Sam. "Mum said we weren't to upset you."

"Oh, that's silly," crooned Gran, stroking her hair. "I won't get upset, I promise. You can tell me anything, and I'll understand."

"If I tell you," said Sam, "will you promise not to let on that you know?"

"I promise," said Gran.

Sam took a deep breath. "It was his bear," she said. "Denzil and I argued about his bear."

"A teddy bear, is it?"

"No. A grizzly."

"Oh. I see."

"The bear's not the only problem. There's a magic charm, which Dad won't give Denzil back. He's stuck here, and even if he could go back to his medieval village he wouldn't, because Valvasor – that's the great wizard who's been teaching Denzil all his magic – is really, *really* angry with him, and doesn't want him back. And the bear's sick and we can't get a vet

101

because it's illegal to have a bear in the first place, and Dad says if anyone finds out we've got one, he'll go to jail."

Gran's face remained perfectly calm and serious, though she blinked a bit. "I think you'd better start the whole story again, dear," she said, "and this time talk slowly, and explain everything. I'm getting a bit slow in my old age."

Quietly, sometimes laughing and sometimes crying, Sam told her everything. At times Gran laughed with her, but mostly she just held Sam's hand very tight, and listened. "And that's the whole awful story," Sam finished, wiping her eyes. "Denzil's in terrible trouble, and I don't know what to do to help him. And when we had our fight, he was going to change me into a toad. That's why my hair's green, probably."

"It's not such an awful colour," said Gran, patting Sam's hand. "And there's no problem that can't be straightened out with a good talk. You and Denzil will sort things out. True friends always do. And why don't you get Valvasor to come and talk to your father?"

"Dad can't meet Valvasor," explained Sam patiently, "because Valvasor's back in medieval England, in a village called Northwood."

"Oh, I forgot that little detail," muttered Gran, biting her lip. "Isn't there any way at all you could contact Valvasor? I mean, there are more ways of making contact with people, than by just picking up a phone, or posting a letter . . . "

102

Suddenly Sam sat bolt upright, her face aglow. "Oh, Gran, you're wonderful!" she cried. "Yes – there is a way! There's an old lady who lives just outside Denzil's village, and I stayed with her once. Mother Wyse, her name is. They say she's a witch, but she isn't really. She's just strange, and very clever. She knows all about making connections across time and space. She taught me how to make a Connecting-Word."

"*You* stayed in a medieval village?" murmured Gran, her eyes like saucers. "You stayed with a *witch*?"

"Yes – no. Not a witch. Oh, Gran! If I could talk to her – to Mother Wyse – she'd talk to Valvasor, and tell him that Denzil's sorry for whatever he did! She would explain everything, and Valvasor would listen to her, because they're true friends!"

"You went back . . . ?" murmured Gran. Then she collapsed on the pillows, her hand against her heart. "I'm feeling a bit tired, sweetheart," she whispered, closing her eyes. "I think you'd better tell me about that another time."

"I'm sorry," said Sam, standing up. Gran looked very pale, and a little vein in her neck was pulsing madly. "I'm sorry," whispered Sam again, distressed. "I've upset you."

"Oh, no, dear, you didn't upset me at all," said Gran, opening her eyes again, and twinkling them at Sam. "You've given me something wonderful to think about. You reminded me of a friend of mine. She once stayed in an old house in England, and saw a ghost.

The ghost was a beautiful young woman, not frightening or horrible at all. My friend saw her as plainly as I see you now. Sometimes I think there are more things in heaven and earth than we know about – and sometimes there are windows between the places, and we can see through."

Sam bent over and kissed her grandmother's cheek. "Goodnight, Gran," she said. "I love you. I hope you get better soon."

"I love you, too, sweetheart," said Gran. "Now don't you worry about your cat. Or your friend. Everything will work out all right in the end. It always does."

They hugged, and Sam went out to the garage to make peace with Denzil. To her surprise, he was asleep, curled up on the garage floor with his head on Wimpy's shoulder. They both were snoring softly.

Sam sat down on the tool-box just inside the garage door. The garage was dim with shadows, and very quiet. It was just getting dark outside, and a full moon glimmered through the garage window, turning the bear's fur blue-black, and making Denzil's silk dress shimmer like scarlet water. His hair mingled with the bear's fur, and his face was very pale against the dark. He looked so strange, so other-worldly, so old and young all at once.

"I'm sorry we fought, Denzil," whispered Sam, even though he was asleep. "I didn't mean what I said. I know you're not too scared to use your magic. But since you won't call Valvasor to come and help us, I have to call someone else . . . "

Then she closed her eyes and concentrated hard. Into her mind came the image of old Mother Wyse, bent and wrinkled and birdlike, with her wild grey hair and lively, beady eyes. Sam thought of the old woman's croaky voice, and the way she got things mixed up because she did not hear very well. Valvasor had introduced Sam as Samantha, which was her proper name, but Mother Wyse had mis-heard, and always called Sam Agapantha. She smiled to herself, remembering.

Sam pictured Mother Wyse the first time she saw her in Valvasor's cottage, bent over with her back to the fire, skirts and petticoats hitched up around her waist, warming her frozen britches. She had been like an excited chicken, clucking and cackling to herself as the fire warmed her, with her skinny legs hopping about in their wrinkled red stockings.

Then Sam remembered visiting Mother Wyse's cottage, dim with smoke and with the wind whistling through the cracks and around the ancient stones. In her mind she saw the furs hanging on the walls, and the shelves with their strange jars, gleaming skulls, and cages of little animals. She saw Mother Wyse bending over her old black cauldron, stirring rabbit stew. Her unruly hair was smoky grey and messier than a big bird's nest, her black eyes burned with strange wisdoms, and her one tooth glinted in the firelight.

While Sam watched, the old woman sniffed the contents of the spoon, muttered something to herself, and began stirring again. The picture of her was so clear that Sam could hear her muttering, and could smell the smoke and the herbs cooking in the stew. It was almost as if she were in the room with Mother Wyse.

"Mother Wyse," she whispered, her voice urgent and low. "Mother Wyse! Will you stop cooking, and listen?"

Mother Wyse lifted her head, and her sharp gaze flashed around the cottage.

"Mother Wyse!" whispered Sam again.

Mother Wyse took the spoon out of the cauldron and set it carefully on the edge of the firepit, where a black cat, waiting hopefully for some stew, licked it clean. Mother Wyse stood very still, her head on one side as she listened. "Is someone calling?" she asked softly, her old voice cracked and wavering.

"I am! It's me! Sam! I need your help!"

"Need more kelp?" muttered Mother Wyse, looking alarmed. "Is that you, Valvasor? Are you down on the coast, rowing around in that dreadful little boat of yours again? Well, I won't come and help you get more kelp! Not in this weather! I know it's wonderful for certain spells, but I refuse –"

"Not Valvasor! It's Sam!" Sam cried softly, afraid of waking Denzil and breaking the connection. But she remembered that Mother Wyse did not hear very well, and got things mixed up sometimes. "It's Sam! Samantha! Remember me?"

"Agapantha?" shrieked Mother Wyse, throwing up her hands in excitement, and startling a crow that sat perched on the bedpost across the room. "Oh,

106

Agapantha! Why didn't you say? What is it you want, dearie?"

Sam almost laughed aloud in her excitement. "Your help, Mother Wyse," she whispered. "I need your *help*."

Inside the MacAllister home, all was unusually quiet. Mr and Mrs MacAllister were still out on their walk, and Travis was in the lounge by himself watching television. Theresa had gone into her parents' room to make a phone call. She had been there ever since Adam had left, talking to the same person for an hour, laughing often, her voice soft and low.

Murgatroyd had gnawed his way through a packet of peanuts in the pantry, and was taking refuge under the sheets in Mr MacAllister's side of the bed, where he considered himself relatively safe from Joplin, and in danger only of being squashed if Theresa moved and sat on him. And Joplin . . .

Joplin was where he had been all the time: he was on Theresa's dressing-table, crouched over an opened box of chocolates, eating the ones that smelled interesting, and dribbling over the rest. He had knocked over several things, including a vase of beautiful red rosebuds, and the spilled water had ruined the extravagant Valentine's Day card from someone called Charles.

Gran was sleeping soundly, dreaming of medieval villages, grizzly bears, angels, angry wizards, and wonderful, magical old women.

Suddenly a wind swept through Gran's room,

blowing her hair about on the pillow, and tossing the sheet across her face. Gran woke suddenly, struggling to throw the sheet off her face – and her eyes opened wide in astonishment.

Her room was full of light. The light changed, became warm and rosy like a dawn, then the next moment was silver as the moon, shifting to pink again, or gold like a sunset. There was a sound like the wind, and strange distant voices, laughter, people calling, and children singing.

Then, as the light settled into a warm silvery-grey like a morning, an extraordinary presence appeared. It was an old woman, tiny and wrinkled, and wreathed in a glowing haze like smoke. A tangled nest of hair floated about her face, and she had marvellous dark eyes that seemed to hold all the wisdom of the universe.

Gran clutched the sheet about her neck and her old heart thundered in awe and amazement. She felt joyful and sad all at once, but not afraid. "Dear angel," she whispered, "is this my time to go?"

The angel lifted her chaotic grey hair out of her eyes, and stared at Gran. "God a-mercy, Agapantha!" she croaked, distraught. "I'm so very sorry. I've arrived a wee bit late, haven't I? Shall I go back, and try again?"

"Oh, no – please!" said Gran. "You could come even later, if you like. I'm in no hurry."

"I thought you were," said the angel.

"No. Not at all."

"You *are* Agapantha, aren't you?" asked the angel,

moving a little closer, and squinting carefully at Gran's face. "It's hard to tell, with you so old now."

"I'm not Agapantha," said Gran, looking relieved. "Violet. My name's Violet. Maybe you got your flowers mixed up."

"Aye, maybe," clucked the angel, scratching her whiskery chin. "I've got something mixed up. More than a few hours, I should think."

Gran suddenly smiled. "Well, I'm glad it's not me you're looking for," she said. "I don't feel ready to die, just yet."

"Ready to fly?" asked the visitor, looking surprised. "You fly?"

"Well, I used to, when I was younger," said Gran. "I had a little plane of my own. Had so much fun in it. I can't fly now, of course. I have a bad heart. Silly thing. It goes frantic at the slightest bit of excitement. It's a bit frantic now, actually." She collapsed back on the pillows, trying to breathe calmly and slowly.

The strange angel sat on the edge of the bed, and put a wrinkled, claw-like hand on Gran's chest. "Yes, I can feel it," she said. "It's leaping around like a flea in a frenzy. What you need, madam, is a good dose of hawthorn with a sprinkling of hag taper. That's the best thing for a sick heart. I'll just pop back and get you some, then I'll look for Agapantha again."

"Thank you," murmured Gran, with a pale smile.

There was an explosion of light and a sound like distant thunder, and the visitor vanished. Gran lay in the darkness, praying quietly. After a while the angel reappeared, holding a dark green bottle with a glass stopper. She took the stopper out, and Gran smelled something foul. "It won't taste very nice," the angel said, putting the bottle to Gran's lips and helping her to take a sip, "but it will work miracles. Absolute miracles. Here – I'll leave the bottle on your table, and you can drink a few sips thrice a day."

"Thank you," said Gran, trying not to pull a face at the taste. "You're very kind. Not at all what I expected an angel to look like, but very kind, just the same."

"Oh, I'm not blind, madam," said the visitor, patting Gran's hand and standing up to go. "Just hard-of-hearing occasionally. Do you mind if I make a little spell, and find Agapantha from here? I feel that she's very close. It won't take a moment."

"That's quite all right," said Gran. "Only I do feel sorry for her. I hope she's had a good life."

"Oh, she will," said the angel, confidently. "She'll make a very good wife for someone, one day. So long as they do what they're told, and don't argue with her. Actually, I am rather hoping that one day, when they're older, she and Denzil might . . . But there are one or two little difficulties . . . Now, what spell do I need . . . "

The angel muttered to herself for a while, and Gran closed her eyes. She was feeling very relaxed and calm, and already her heart had improved and was beating strongly and steadily. She opened her eyes to thank the heavenly visitor once more, but she was gone. Gran sighed and closed her eyes again.

"Thank you, dear God," she whispered, into the peaceful dark. "Your ways certainly are mysterious, but very wonderful."

Then she dropped instantly into a deep and healing sleep.

9 The Connecting-Word

am sat on the edge of the tool-box in the dim garage, whispering Mother Wyse's name. She could no longer see Mother Wyse – it was as if the Connecting-Word had worked for a few moments, then been broken. Mother Wyse's face kept getting mixed up with Gran's, and Sam couldn't concentrate any more. Also, she realised she wanted to go to the toilet. She got up, opened the garage door quietly so she wouldn't wake Denzil or the bear, and went back inside. She went to the toilet, then to the bathroom to wash her hands. While there, she caught a glimpse of herself in the mirror – and stared, flabbergasted. Her hair *was* green! She was shocked at first, then decided she liked it, and shook her curls and looked at them from different angles, admiring the different shades of emerald, olive, and golden-green. Suddenly she smelled smoke. Alarmed, she stood sniffing, then realised that the smoke was scented heavily with stew and herbs.

"Mother Wyse!" she whispered.

The smell of smoke got stronger, and the room glowed as if on fire. Then, out of the smoke and rosy light, stepped Mother Wyse. "Agapantha, dearie!" the old woman shrieked, flinging her arms around Sam. "Found you!"

Sam hugged her back, laughing with joy. "I'm so glad you're here!" she said. "I was afraid the Connecting-Word hadn't worked."

"Gone berserk?" cackled Mother Wyse, surprised. "Oh dearie, my Connections never go berserk. Well ... not often, anyway. How be you, dearie? Besides your hair turning green."

"I'm fine, but –" Sam stopped, and glanced over Mother Wyse's shoulder. The bathroom door was open, and along the dark passage she could see the lounge door. It was closed, but the light shone underneath, and she could hear the TV going. She could also hear voices in the kitchen, and realised that her parents had arrived home. Quickly, Sam wriggled out of Mother Wyse's smoky embrace, closed the bathroom door, and locked it. "We'll have to be quiet," she whispered.

"What was that, dearie?" shouted Mother Wyse.

"I said – we'll have to be quiet!" whispered Sam again, close to Mother Wyse's ear.

"Riot?" croaked Mother Wyse, alarmed, looking all around. "Where's the riot?"

"Here, soon, if we don't keep our voices down!" said Sam. She took Mother Wyse's hands and gazed earnestly into her face. "Please listen carefully," she said. "Denzil's here, with a bear. Valvasor's fired him, and he won't go back. Will you talk to Valvasor, explain that Denzil's really sorry, and he was only –"

113

"Sam?" called Mr MacAllister, from outside the bathroom door. "What are you and Denzil doing in there?" He tried to open the door, found it locked, and muttered angrily. Then he shouted, "It's no use locking yourself in there, Denzil, just because you refuse to find Valvasor for me! You'll have to come out sooner or later, so it might as well be now, while I'm only moderately furious!"

"Accuse and blind Valvasor!" muttered Mother Wyse, shocked. "Oh, I know he's upset the three spinsters, but there's no need to poke out his eyes!"

Sam clapped her hand over Mother Wyse's mouth, and called loudly, "We're cleaning our teeth." She turned on a bathroom tap, hard. "And after that we're having a bath."

"Not together, you're not!" yelled Mr MacAllister.

"I'm just running the bath for Denzil!" called Sam. "I'll be out soon."

Then she heard her mother's voice, sounding bewildered. "But he just had a bath this afternoon. What's going on, Sam?"

"Nothing!" yelled Sam.

"Well, while you're doing nothing, be quick about it!" called her father. "I want to have a shower."

They went away, and Sam whispered frantically, "You have to listen carefully, Mother Wyse."

Mother Wyse was busy looking all around the bathroom, marvelling at the strange smooth painted walls, the shining white bath and shower, and the bright tiles on the floor. Then she noticed the mirror, and leaned forward to inspect it. An extraordinary old

114

crone peered back at her, and Mother Wyse shrieked in astonishment. Frantically, Sam tried to hush her, explaining that it was a mirror.

"Holy saints – 'tis myself, I see!" breathed Mother Wyse, enthralled. Then she smiled her one-toothed smile, and patted down her hair.

Sam put her hands on the old woman's shoulders, making her pay attention. "Please listen," she said. "My father wants to see Valvasor. Can you arrange it?"

"Rearrange it?" asked Mother Wyse, looking puzzled, and tearing her eyes away from the wondrous mirror. "Rearrange what, dearie?"

"My father wants to see Valvasor," said Sam, speaking very clearly though she kept her voice low. "Will you ask Valvasor to come here?"

Mother Wyse shook her head, muttering. "Valvasor doesn't wish to disappear," she said. "'Tis his apprentice who's disappeared. We can't all just vanish off the land, dearie. There'd be no-one left. Mind you, he's in a bit of trouble, is Valvasor, and disappearing for a while might be prudent."

"Denzil's here," whispered Sam. "With a bear."

"A bare what?"

"A grizzly. From a fair."

Mother Wyse nodded slowly, though she still looked mystified. "He's not had that problem before," she said. "I suppose that's why he disappeared, so Valvasor wouldn't see it."

"That's right," said Sam, relieved that the old woman understood at last.

"What do you want me to do?" asked Mother Wyse.

"Talk to Valvasor. Ask him to forgive Denzil. Ask him to take him back. Do you understand? Please understand."

"You want me to talk to Valvasor?" asked Mother Wyse. "Why didn't you say so in the first place, dearie? Of course I'll talk to him. I'll tell him all about Weasel and his frizzy hair. Though frizzy hair isn't as frightful as green hair. What have you two been doing?"

"Not his hair. His *bear*. His grizzly *bear*."

"Frizzy bear. He's got a frizzy bear. Oh, dear. "

"That's near enough," muttered Sam to herself, thinking that contacting Mother Wyse wasn't such a good idea after all. She added, as loudly as she dared, "Ask Valvasor to forgive him."

"Give him what?"

"*Forgive!*" cried Sam, exasperated. "To *forgive* him!"

"Sam!" called Mr MacAllister, from outside the door. "Will you two stop arguing, and hurry up, or do I have to break down this door!"

Mother Wyse lifted her head, and murmured in a worried way, "Shakedown with Valvasor? Oh, Sam, 'tis a right pickle Valvasor's in! I'd best be off now, to help him. I'll come back soon."

"No!" cried Sam, but it was too late. Mother Wyse vanished.

Sam turned off the bathroom tap, and opened the door.

"About time!" said her father, irritably. He poked his head into the bathroom, and waited. "Well, where's Denzil?" he asked.

"Denzil?" repeated Sam, looking cool.

"He was in there with you."

"No he wasn't. I was by myself."

"You were talking to someone."

"No. I was just talking to myself in the mirror, practising different voices. Like you do, when you're rehearsing for a play."

Mr MacAllister's eyes grew narrow, and he looked from the empty bathroom to Sam's innocent face, and back to the bathroom again. He went in and searched behind the shower curtain, then in the large basket where the dirty linen was kept. He looked at the window, checked that it was locked, then glanced behind the curtains. Frowning, he even looked down the plug hole in the bath. While he was looking there, Sam fled into her room and slammed the door. Quickly she changed into pyjamas, got into bed, then lay for a while biting her lower lip, and worrying.

She heard Theresa's bedroom door close and her radio go on, and then Theresa gave a wail of rage. The next moment Sam's door flew open and Theresa stood there, red in the face and spitting fury. "Where's your rat?" demanded Theresa. She was so angry, she didn't even notice Sam's hair.

"I don't know," said Sam.

"Well, if I find him, you'll be sorry," said Theresa. "He's been eating my chocolates, the ones I got for Valentine's Day. He's dribbled all over them, the

117

filthy little beggar. And he knocked over my roses and ruined my special card."

"I thought Adam gave you a book about fixing motors," said Sam.

Theresa went redder, and said haughtily, "It's none of your business."

"If you get another boyfriend," said Sam, "I'll tell him how you and Adam sit in his car for hours and hours, sucking each other's face."

"See if I care," said Theresa, going out.

"And I'll tell him about the boxer underpants you gave Adam for his birthday!" Sam yelled after her. "The smooth ones with little pink elephants and –"

"How do you know about those?" cried Theresa, coming in again, blue eyes blazing.

"I found them hidden under your bed, before you gave them to him," said Sam serenely, "when I was looking for Murgatroyd once."

"You little snoop!" hissed Theresa. "You can't be trusted, can you? I'm going to get a great big rat-trap, and hide it in my room. Then I'll catch Murgatroyd – or you. Either victim would be satisfying."

"You could try catching a new boyfriend in it," said Sam. "It's the only way you'll get one, with your face."

"Shows how much you know!" snorted Theresa. "I've already got one." Then she stuck her beautiful nose in the air, and flounced out.

Sam sighed, and picked up a book. She had just finished half a page, when there was a quiet knock on her door and her mother came in. "Are you all right, love?" she asked, sitting on Sam's bed. Then she noticed Sam's hair. "Oh, Sam!" she cried. "What on earth have you done?"

Sam went bright pink, and thought quickly. "Denzil and I found Dad's box of theatre makeup," she said. "There was some hair dye in it. Denzil dared me."

Her mother shook her head, and laughed a little. "I suppose it'll wash out easily enough. Green hair's a minor disaster, when I've got a wizard and a bear and a very sick grandmother to worry about. Where is Denzil, by the way? Is he asleep in your tree-house?"

"He's in the garage with Wimpy."

"Will he be safe?"

"Oh, Denzil won't hurt him. He won't even use magic on him any more."

"I meant," smiled Mrs MacAllister, "will *Denzil* be safe?"

Sam grinned. "The way they were curled up asleep together, I think the only things that are going to bite Denzil are the fleas."

"We'll have to give both of them a good dusting with flea powder, in the morning," said Mrs MacAllister. She leaned down and gave Sam a hug and a kiss. "Goodnight, darling. And try not to worry about Denzil too much. He'll work everything out."

"But what if he can't get Valvasor to come and see Dad?" asked Sam. "Will Dad really keep the magic charm? Because if he does, Denzil can never go back."

"I don't think that will happen," said her mother. "I had a big talk to your father tonight, while we were out walking. He's going to try to be more tolerant. I know he's been very grumpy lately, dear, but there's something he's worrying about . . . "

"Well, what?" asked Sam. "If he's worried about money and stuff, he shouldn't take it out on us. Especially Denzil. Denzil doesn't even know what money is."

"It's not that," said her mother, quietly. "I wasn't going to tell you, but I suppose you're old enough to know these things. Your father's eyesight is failing rather rapidly, and . . . Well, he doesn't need other things to worry about, on top of that."

"Is he going blind?" asked Sam, her voice catching in her throat.

"We don't know. He has an appointment to see a specialist, but it's a month away yet. In the meantime, he just doesn't need added stress in his life."

"Is that why he was trying on Gran's glasses the other day?" asked Sam.

"Was he? The doctor doesn't think glasses will help him, Sam. It's something inside his eyes, that's going wrong. We just have to be patient, and see what the specialist says."

Her mother went out, and Sam picked up her book again. She had almost finished another page when suddenly there was a tremendous yell from somewhere else in the house, and she heard her father shouting. "Get out of here! Out! Out!"

Sam sat bolt upright, horrified. Mother Wyse! Mother Wyse must have arrived in the bathroom again, while Mr MacAllister was in the shower!

Sam listened to all the noise, her eyes wide. She could hear her father yelling again, loud enough to wake the whole neighbourhood, and her mother trying to calm him down. She heard Travis's voice, calm and steady and laughing in that quiet way Travis had. When it was peaceful again, Sam lay down, put the book under her pillow, and waited for Mother Wyse to burst in.

But it was Travis who came in, with Joplin in his arms. With a cry of joy, Sam leapt out of bed and gathered Joplin close, kissing his ears and the top of his head. "Oh, you wicked cat!" she said. "You've got chocolate all over your face!"

"I found him slinking out of Theresa's room," smiled Travis, "when she was in here ranting about Murgatroyd eating all her chocolates. I guess Joplin heard her coming, and hid. He's pretty cunning for a cat, isn't he?"

"He's superexcellent," said Sam, poking Joplin between her sheets, and climbing into the bed after him. "What was Dad yelling about?"

"Murgatroyd," said Travis, laughing. "Dad was getting into bed, and got bitten on the toe by Murgatroyd. He wasn't hurt. I've put him in the cage in your tree-house."

Sam giggled. "Poor Dad," she said. "He won't like living in a cage."

Travis chuckled, and ruffled her green curls. "Well, we've got the family zoo all safe and sound," he said. "By the way, I like your hair. Green suits you."

"Travis?" Sam said, suddenly serious. "What *does*

happen to all the animals that go missing? Are they being poisoned?"

"They're being stolen, Sam," Travis told her. "A black truck's been seen driving slowly around the streets at night, and dogs were heard barking inside it. It's been seen by several people, but the police haven't been able to track it down yet."

"Why does someone want to steal animals?" asked Sam, afraid. "What do they do with them?"

Travis didn't reply.

"They're not doing something awful, are they?" Sam whispered. "They're not skinning them for fur coats, or making them into sausages, or something?"

Travis stood up, ruffled her hair again, and bent and kissed her forehead. "Just keep Joplin inside, okay?" he said. Then he grinned. "Trust our family to get it all back-to-front," he said. "Everyone else is losing animals, and we find them."

"I bet Dad would rather lose them than find them," said Sam, glumly.

"He's only grumpy because his hand's sore," said Travis. "You wait. Everything will look better in the morning."

But in the morning everything was worse. In the morning, they woke up to discover that the bear was alone in the garage, and obviously suffering.

And Denzil had disappeared.

10 Magic, Modified Molecules, and a Monkey

reakfast was subdued that morning, at the MacAllister's house. Everyone sat around the table looking worried, and no one felt like eating. Mr MacAllister had picked up the morning paper, squinted at it for a few moments, then folded it up and thrown it on the floor. Travis made a milkshake for Sam, and a big pot of tea for everyone else. Mrs MacAllister sat holding her husband's good hand, and for once Theresa didn't tell them to stop behaving like teenagers.

Sam's hair had miraculously turned back to its own colour during the night, but she was too worried about Denzil to notice. She kept remembering how she had said she wished he'd disappear – and now that he had, she thought it was her fault. But there was another thing, even worse, that worried her.

"You don't think they've stolen him, do you?" Sam asked, in a small voice. "Those people in the black truck. They haven't got Denzil?"

"I doubt it, Sam," said Travis. "They steal animals, not wizards in red silk dresses."

"But they might have," whispered Sam, "if he'd turned himself into a dog again."

Her father grunted scornfully, but everyone else was very quiet. Then Adam arrived, and they told him about Denzil.

"He'll turn up; he's probably just popped home to sort things out with Valvasor," said Adam, trying to look cheerful. He sat down by Theresa, put his arm around her neck, and moved to kiss her lips. But she turned away, and he kissed her ear instead.

"I didn't know you were coming this morning," Theresa said.

"I didn't know I needed an invitation," he replied, puzzled by her cool manner. "What's wrong, babe?"

"Nothing," she said. "And don't call me babe. I hate it. And Denzil hasn't gone home to Valvasor. He can't, since Dad's got his medallion."

Adam sighed, and nodded. "I forgot," he said. "But, talking of jewellery ... I bought another Valentine's present for you, since you didn't like your book." He took a small red box from his pocket, and gave it to Theresa.

Without a word she untied the ribbon, and opened it. It was half of a tiny silver heart, fixed to a silver chain and engraved with her name.

"I'm wearing the other half," said Adam, touching a chain on his neck that was newer than all the others. "I thought I couldn't go wrong this time, with jewellery, since we both like it."

"We can all see that *you* like it," muttered Mr MacAllister, eyeing Adam's silver earrings, chains, and bracelets. "It's a wonder you can stand upright, with all that metal on."

Theresa put the heart half on the table, and pushed it away from her. "It's nice," she said.

"Is that all?" asked Adam, hurt. "*Nice?* Don't you like it?"

"We're all worried about Denzil, Adam," said Mrs MacAllister, softly. "Wrong timing, maybe."

Adam grinned and nodded, but the hurt stayed in his eyes.

Sam shot Theresa a furious look, and went out to the garage to check Wimpy. He was sitting up like a human child, licking the burnt pads of his front paws, and swaying his head from side to side as if he were in pain. He cringed away when he saw her, but she spoke softly and very gently stroked his back. Reassured, Wimpy sniffed her cheek and hair, then went back to swaying his huge head, grunting softly. His infected eye was almost closed, and there were flies buzzing about the ulcers on his neck. Sam shooed them away, and stood up to go back inside. She hated leaving Wimpy; in spite of his size he was still only a young bear, hurt and bewildered and alone. In tears, Sam went back into the kitchen. "We have to take him to the vet," she told everyone. "He's in pain."

"You know we can't do that, darling," said her mother gently. "I don't know what we can do for him.

125

Whoever we ask to help is bound to report us for having an illegal animal, and we could be fined thousands of dollars."

"Or I could end up in prison," said Mr MacAllister. "Mind you, prison might be restful, after this place."

Gran waltzed into the kitchen, humming softly to herself. "Good morning, all!" she said cheerfully.

They looked up, astonished. Gran usually had breakfast in bed, and stayed there to rest until the afternoon. But here she was, sparkly-eyed and pink-cheeked, and with a spring in her step that they hadn't seen for a long time.

"Well, I thought you'd all be pleased now that I'm feeling better," she said, looking at their solemn faces.

"We are pleased, Mum," said Mrs MacAllister, getting up and giving her a hug. "It's lovely to see you looking so well. But Denzil's gone missing, and we've no idea where he is."

"Perhaps he's just gone home," said Gran, sitting at the table and pouring herself a cup of tea.

"But he's left the bear behind," said Theresa. Then she reddened, thinking that Gran didn't know about the bear, and wasn't supposed to know. "I mean," she stammered, "he's got a bare behind. No trousers. He can't go home without his trousers."

"He could wear his Chinese dress," murmured Gran, sipping her tea, her dark eyes dancing at Sam. "I think he looked rather fine in red silk. I'm sure he'd impress the people in his little town."

Sam grinned, and Gran winked at her.

"What's made you feel so much better, Mum?" asked Mrs MacAllister. "Had a good sleep?"

"Oh, an excellent sleep," smiled Gran.

"*I* could have done with a bit more sleep," muttered Mr MacAllister. "My hand hurt all night, where that bear bit – that bare-faced rat bit me."

"It's a wonder he didn't wake you up, Mum, with all his yelling," said Mrs MacAllister. "Half the neighbourhood must have heard him."

"It must have been a big bite, for a little rat," observed Gran, looking at her son's bandaged hand. "I'd have thought something much bigger bit you."

"He had a good gnaw on me," said Mr MacAllister, and Sam giggled.

"No need for you to laugh, young lady," said her father, raising his good hand and shaking a finger at her. "You'd better keep that rat of yours in its cage, in future. Otherwise it'll end up being used for –"

"Anyone for some toast?" asked Travis, leaping up from the table. "I'm beginning to feel quite hungry."

"End up being used for what?" asked Sam.

At that moment the back door was flung open, and Denzil rushed in. He was wide-eyed and flushed with excitement, and the red Chinese dress was hitched up around his hips because he'd been running fast. The purple tights had fallen half down, but he didn't notice. Neither did anyone else. They were all staring at the thing he was holding in his arms.

Denzil was holding a monkey.

For a few minutes there was a stunned silence. Denzil stared around at them all, his face shining.

127

"See what I found!" he whispered. "Beautiful, is he not?"

"No, he is not," said Mr MacAllister, standing up.

"Oh, he's wonderful!" cried Sam, jumping up and going over to stroke the monkey.

"So cute!" breathed Mrs MacAllister.

"Looks a bit like Denzil himself," smiled Adam.

Denzil gave the monkey to Sam, pulled up the purple tights, smoothed down the red dress, and rearranged the bras about his waist. The bras were full of nuts and apricots, and there was a banana poked down the front of the dress. "For the monkey," explained Denzil, pulling the banana out, and giving it to the animal. The monkey began to peel it, very slowly and carefully, with long and delicate fingers. It crammed half the banana in its mouth and blinked at them all, its cheeks bulging. Then it scratched itself under the armpits, reached out, and helped itself to a nut from Denzil's bras.

"Where did you get that thing?" asked Mr MacAllister, his voice shaking and low.

"From the manor house nearby," said Denzil, jerking his head in the direction of Mr Gump's house. "I got bored, so I changed myself into a mouse, and went in for a look. I found him."

"Liar," said Mr MacAllister.

Denzil looked hurt. "Am not! I was a mouse."

"I don't care if you were a pink baboon with a purple backside," said Mr MacAllister. "You didn't find that monkey in old Gump's house. It's against the law in this country to keep monkeys. They're like bears. Illegal. Old Gump wouldn't have one. You went back home to the circus, didn't you? Helped yourself to another one of Valvasor's beasts, and came back here. What are you bringing us next? An elephant?"

"It's true!" shrieked Denzil, his face getting as red as Mr MacAllister's. "I did find it in that manor house! I haven't been home! I can't go, can I, without the magic charm you burglared off me."

"We'll have none of that crazy talk!" roared Mr MacAllister. "I'm sick of hearing about magic! You're no more a wizard than I am!"

"Am so!" screamed Denzil.

"You are not! You're a thief and a liar!"

"I'll show you!" raged Denzil. "You want to be a toad?"

"No, I do *not* want to be a toad!" yelled Mr MacAllister. "I want to be a bird, then I can fly away from this mad-house whenever I like, and have some peace!"

"If that's your wish, my lord," said Denzil, and started furiously muttering.

> *Great powers of change,*
> *This man doth seek*
> *A full exchange:*
> *For mouth, a beak –*

"No!" cried Sam, but Denzil was too mad to listen. He went on, his eyes blazing with green, unearthly light:

> *In place of arms,*
> *A pair of wings,*

129

And, by my charms,
All bird-like things:
For he would fly
Within the light,
With freedom's cry
And falcon's sight.
So I invoke
The magic law
To grant the hope
That he asked for –
Reform the plan
By his own word,
And change the man
Into a bird.

In front of them all, Mr MacAllister began to change. At first the changes were subtle; just a strange greyness creeping across his skin, and a shifting of his hair into shining feather-shapes. Then his nose began to sharpen and lengthen, and his clothes stirred as if they were alive, changing into sleek black folds. The folds shifted, fluttered, became glossy blue-black feathers. At the same time, Mr MacAllister began to shrink.

Mrs MacAllister went deadly white. Travis was sitting near her, and he put his arm about her shoulders so he could catch her if she fainted. But she didn't faint, just watched in horror as her husband shrank away until he was the size of a turkey. He was almost fully a bird, but he was still wearing his own shoes; and when he stretched his wings and fluttered them, there were fingers on the ends of his flight-feathers. He continued to shrink, and the shoes split into curving strips, turned yellow, and were claws.

Sam watched, clutching the monkey, her eyes out on stalks. Adam was frowning a little, fascinated, wondering about atoms and molecules, and the chemical exchanges that were going on. Theresa rushed out to the toilet, and they heard her being sick.

"It's only magic!" Sam called after her. "It's all right! He's going to turn Dad into himself again!"

Then she glanced at Gran. The old woman was sitting absolutely still, her cup halfway to her mouth as if she were about to take another sip of tea, then had forgotten. Her eyes were fixed on the bird, and she looked as if she were hardly breathing. Sam hoped she wasn't about to have a heart attack. "Are you all right, Gran?" she asked gently.

"Oh, I'm fine, dear," Gran said, tearing her eyes off the bird, and smiling at her. "You told me he was a wizard. Wonderful, isn't he?"

Mrs MacAllister groaned, and Travis held her more tightly. "It's all right, Mum," he said. "It's only an illusion. We're all hypnotised."

Suddenly there was a wild flutter of wings, and the bird flapped up towards the windows. One window was shut, and it flew into it. Sam screamed. The bird fell on to the window sill, stumbled about shaking its head, then stretched its wings again. This time it did a beautiful take-off, straight out of the open window. They saw it drift in a haphazard way across the

131

garden, get tangled up in a rose-bush, squawk angrily, then flutter off again.

"Stop him!" Sam shrieked at Denzil. "He'll kill himself!"

Denzil went over to the open window and peered out. "Nay – he's mastered flight already," he said. And he was right: Mr MacAllister was soaring grandly above the garden, cawing in triumph. Then he rose, hardly flapping his wings, up over the trees, over the garage, and vanished into the blue summer skies.

"Now you've done it!" cried Sam, going over to Denzil, and staring in disbelief at the empty sky. "We'll never get him back now. "

"He'll come home," said Denzil, taking the monkey back, and offering it an apricot. "He'll return – if he wants to."

"What if he can't find his way?" cried Sam. "He's not used to flying! The world looks different from up there! He's a bird now! He probably won't even remember what our house looks like! He'll probably look for a nest in a tree! He could fly for miles! Birds do, you know! They migrate! He could end up in Honolulu!"

Denzil gulped. He had no idea where Honolulu was, but he guessed it wasn't just the other side of the garage roof. "He might like it in Honolulu," he said.

"He probably would," agreed Adam. "All those white beaches, and bars along the shore, and girls in bikinis. He'd think he'd hit Paradise."

Mrs MacAllister gave a little wail, and Travis

hugged her reassuringly. "No he wouldn't, Mum," he said. "He'd hate it. He can't hold a glass of beer with a wing."

Gran finished drinking her tea, and put the cup down. It rattled slightly in the saucer. Sam went and stood beside her, putting an arm about Gran's neck. "I hope this doesn't frighten you too much, Gran," she whispered.

"Oh, no dear," murmured Gran, patting her hand. "It's all quite wonderful, really. Here I am, almost eighty years old, and I'm only just beginning to see."

"But you've always been able to see, Gran."

"Yes, but not *these* things," said Gran, her voice hushed with awe. "Not these miraculous, mystical things. These things beyond our understanding."

"It's not so difficult to understand, really, Gran," said Adam, smiling at her, his silver earrings glinting in the morning sun. "It's to do with molecular structure, chemical reactions, molecules being modified, subatomic mathematics, and that sort of thing."

"Oh," said Gran, blinking. "Does that cover angels, too?"

"I'm not sure about them," said Adam. "Probably beings from another dimension altogether."

"Yes, that's what I thought," said Gran, eagerly. "And they don't all wear white dresses and play harps, you know. They don't have wings either, which is rather disappointing. I was looking forward to – "

"Oh, Mum," groaned Mrs MacAllister, "your only

son's turned into a magpie, and you go on about *angels*?"

"Not a magpie, a falcon," said Denzil, cramming his mouth full of the monkey's apricots. "There's a difference."

"Do you think Dad will end up an angel?" asked Sam, in a small voice.

"No. His wings are the wrong colour," said Denzil. "Besides, he's flying, not dying."

"This is nothing to joke about, Denzil," said Travis.

"I'm not joking!" cried Denzil, spraying half-chewed apricot all over them. "I'm serious! I don't know why you're all so upset! He *asked* to be a bird! I didn't do anything against his own will! I never broke the Great Laws!"

He stormed off out of the door, and Sam yelled after him, "Where are you going?"

"To the manor house over there!" he shouted back. "I'm taking the monkey back. Then I'm going to see Wimpy."

Sam rushed over to her mother. "Don't worry, Mum," she said. "Denzil will get Dad back. If he doesn't, I'll punch his lights out."

"Thank you darling, that's a great comfort to me," said her mother, with a small smile.

"You go with Denzil," said Travis, getting up and patting Sam's shoulder. "I'll settle things down here. Maybe Denzil could change . . . you know . . . buzz off and look for Dad."

"Maybe I could go with him," said Sam eagerly, and hurried out after Denzil.

"How are you going to put the monkey back?" asked Sam, as they entered Mr Gump's property.

"Gawd, you're dumb!" Denzil said, looking at her sideways. "Same way I took it out. I'll walk through the door into the manor house, and just put it back."

"But what if Mr Gump sees you?"

"He won't. He's not there."

Sam heaved a sigh of relief, and followed Denzil as he pushed the front door open and went inside. Sam had never been in Mr Gump's house before, and she looked around, astonished.

The walls were covered with paintings of animals! There were pictures of lions and elephants, parrots and snakes, monkeys and zebras, baboons and armadillos. There was a rug on the floor with a tiger on it, and in one corner stood a splendid carving of a giraffe, so high it almost reached the ceiling. There were carvings of birds all over a large cupboard, and the fabric on the sofa and chairs was designed to look like leopard skin.

"Wow!" breathed Sam.

Denzil went over to a little perch in one corner of the room, and sat the monkey on it. There was a fine chain on the perch, and a tiny hook that fixed on to a ring on the monkey's leg. Denzil attached the monkey to its perch the way it had been when he found it, and turned to go. He noticed Sam staring at all the pictures, and grinned.

"I was here ages, looking at his walls," Denzil said. "There are some mighty peculiar creatures here. This, for instance." He pointed to a painting of an elephant, and shook his head in wonder. "Whoever made *that* up had a good imagination," he said. "It's weirder than a dragon."

But Sam was looking at black and white photos on a shelf, and didn't hear Denzil. There were dozens of photos, all of animals – but not ordinary ones. These were zoo animals. And in nearly every picture was the same man – a young man whose face looked vaguely familiar – and he was inside the enclosures with the animals, feeding them or hugging them or just peacefully being with them. There were pictures of him holding baby gorillas, wolf-cubs, and newly-hatched alligators. There were pictures of snakes draped over him, large lizards crawling up his arms, and emus and elephants looking over his shoulder. Sam's favourite was a picture of him lying in some grass hugging a tiger, and the huge cat was hugging him back, and looking not fierce at all, but benevolent and beautiful.

Suddenly there was a stamping outside the door, and, to her horror, Mr Gump came in. He was carrying a bag of groceries. He saw the visitors, and the bag of groceries crashed to the floor. "Little thieves!" he roared. "I've caught you red-handed!"

Immediately Denzil began saying a disappearing spell, but he changed his mind. If he disappeared, Sam would call him a milksop again. So he stood his ground, stuck out his chin, and tried to think up a good excuse for being here.

Sam thought of one first. "We're not stealing anything, Mr Gump," she said. "Mum sent us."

"What for?" asked Mr Gump suspiciously, moving his feet because egg yolk was seeping out of the busted grocery bag and getting under his shoes.

"Aye, what for?" asked Denzil, looking at Sam.

Sam glared at Denzil, then smiled sweetly at Mr Gump and said, "My mother apologises most sincerely, but we can't pay the money we owe. Not just yet."

"I told her she's got till the end of the week," growled Mr Gump. "Now get out." Suddenly he noticed the apricots and nuts packed into the pouches of the strange belt Denzil wore. "You *are* a thief!" cried Mr Gump, his eyebrows twitching dangerously.

"Am not!" said Denzil, haughtily. "I'm a burglar!"

"I like your photos, Mr Gump," said Sam, to change the subject. "That's you, isn't it, with the animals? I love that one of you with the tiger. It must be wonderful, to hug a tiger."

To her astonishment, all the fury and outrage vanished from Mr Gump's face, and he actually smiled. "Yes, it is wonderful," he said, his voice suddenly surprisingly soft. "I loved my years at the zoo."

"The zoo?" asked Sam, curious. "You worked at a zoo?"

"Yes, I did, as a matter of fact. Those were the happiest years of my life. I loved it there, with all the animals. They're much better than people, you know. Animals are. They don't hurt you like people do. Unconditional love. That's what animals give."

"What did you do at the zoo?" asked Sam. "Did you

137

feed the animals?"

"I worked out their diets for them, but I only fed them if they were sick. I was the zoo vet."

A huge excitement went through Sam. "The *vet?*" she whispered.

Mr Gump nodded.

Sam tried to calm herself, though her heart hammered in her ribs, and she hoped desperately that she wasn't making a terrible mistake. "Did you ever look after bears?" she asked.

"Sometimes," said Mr Gump, looking at the photographs with a faraway look in his eyes. "I've looked after most animals, at some time or other."

Sam took a deep breath. "Mr Gump, we need a vet. We've got a sick animal at home."

"Won't your own vet see it?" asked Mr Gump.

"No, he won't," said Sam, and Mr Gump looked shocked.

"He said it's an eagle, but it isn't," explained Denzil.

"Illegal, not an eagle," said Sam.

"It's got to have parchments," said Denzil.

"Papers and a passport," said Sam.

"And I should have taken it to a disintegration place, but I took it straight to Sam's," added Denzil.

"He means immigration," said Sam.

"What on earth have you got over there?" asked Mr Gump, his eyebrows going crazy.

"A bear," said Sam and Denzil together.

"A koala?"

"A grizzly," said Sam.

"With burnt feet," added Denzil. "I saved it from a fair. They made it dance on a hot plate."

Mr Gump's eyebrows shot so high, Sam thought they were going to fly right off his face. "Good Lord – I thought that kind of thing went out with the Middle Ages!" Mr Gump cried. "Go home, children! I'll gather up a few bandages and ointments and antibiotics, and I'll be over!"

11 The Vet

"We've found a vet!" yelled Sam, racing inside.

Denzil was close behind, his silk dress hitched up around his knees. "He's bringing over some bandages and ointments, and some scanty chaotics!" he shouted.

"Well, we surely could do with a few more chaotics," said Adam.

Shakily, Mrs MacAllister stood up. "I'm very pleased there's some good news," she said. "Who is it? Not our vet?"

"It's Mr Gump!" announced Sam, smiling. "He's a vet, and we didn't know! He used to work in a zoo."

"He'll know how to treat Wimpy, then!" said Travis. "What a stroke of luck!"

"He'll report us, though, for sure," said Mrs MacAllister, looking worried.

"I don't think he will," said Travis, with a sly look in his dark eyes. "I don't think he's in a position to do that."

"He's coming!" said Denzil, looking out the back door. "He's got a big bag!"

"Take him out to the garage, then," said Mrs MacAllister. "I'll be there shortly." She looked at Gran, and gave a wan smile. "I think you'd better go back to bed, Mum," she said. "There's too much excitement for you, around here. I'm worried about your heart."

"Did someone say there's a vet here?" asked Theresa, coming back into the kitchen. Her face was still very pale. "We didn't get a vet for Dad, did we?" Suddenly her voice rose in panic. "He's all right, isn't he? He hasn't flown into a window? Has he hurt himself? Oh God, has Joplin got him?"

"The vet's for Wimpy," explained her mother, with an uneasy glance at Gran. "Please, Mum, go and lie down. I'm so afraid your heart – "

"My heart's fine," said Gran, standing up. "And the excitement is actually good for me. Stimulates my adrenalin. But I'll go and rest, if it'll make you feel better."

"It would," said Mrs MacAllister.

So Gran went to her room, and everyone else went out to the garage. Outside, Adam caught Theresa's hand, and stopped her beside his car.

"What's wrong, Theresa?" he asked, putting his arms about her and drawing her close. "You're in a strange mood. Awfully quiet."

"What do you expect?" she snapped, pulling away. "My father's just been turned into a bird. Am I supposed to hire a band and throw a party?"

"You know what I mean. You've been quiet towards me, even before your father's

141

metamorphosis. And you won't let me near you. Something's happened, hasn't it? Have you met someone else?"

She gazed out across the garden, biting her lip, and blinking back tears. "I don't want to hurt you," she said.

"That means you're going to, so you might as well get it over and done with. Don't string me along, Theresa, or lie to me. Just tell me straight. Who is he?"

"Charles Prendergast."

Adam sighed heavily. He knew Charles Prendergast; knew he had already been to court for dangerous driving, but his wealthy father had paid for a cunning lawyer and got the case dismissed. But he didn't tell Theresa that; he just kissed her cheek, and said, "I wish you happiness. I really do. And I'm always here, if you need me. All you have to do is phone. Take care, babe."

She started to say something angry, then stopped, smiling a little. Her smile faded as she watched him drive away, and her eyes were wet as she went into the garage.

Mr Gump had already begun examining Wimpy. In silence the MacAllisters stood around and watched. Wimpy was lying with his nose across his front paws, his eyes half closed and his side rising and falling quickly as he panted. He did not even lift his head as Mr Gump moved his hands gently over him, looking into his ears, inspecting the pads of his burned feet, and lifting his eyelids to peer into his glazed eyes. He looked at Wimpy's teeth, and examined his gums and tongue. And all the time Mr Gump talked quietly, sometimes to himself and sometimes to Wimpy, his usually harsh voice low and tender. The MacAllisters were astounded at the change in the man: they were used to seeing him all fired up and cranky and complaining; now he was transformed – gentle, loving, and serene. It was wonderful to watch the way he touched Wimpy and talked to him. Every move was full of care, and slow so the bear would not be frightened. And even when Mr Gump's fingers touched a place that hurt, and he made Wimpy grunt with pain, the bear did not snap or snarl. It was as if Wimpy knew the man was trying to help. Sam cried while she watched, feeling as if she were witnessing a miracle. "Please, please let Wimpy be all right," she whispered. Denzil heard, and slipped his hand into hers.

At last Mr Gump stood up. "He's suffering from malnutrition," he said to no one in particular, his eyes still lovingly on the bear. "His burns are infected, and he needs antibiotics. Fortunately I have them. He's also got abrasions on his neck. He's been dragged around roughly by a rope, I should think. And his liver is swollen. He's probably been beaten or kicked at some time. With a bit of tender loving care, some careful grooming, and good food, I think he'll recover splendidly."

"What should we give him to eat?" asked Mrs MacAllister.

"Raw meat, liver, green vegetables, and multivitamins," replied Mr Gump. "I'll make up a mixture for you." He crouched down by Wimpy again and opened the bag he had brought. He took out a bottle with a rubber top and a large syringe with a vicious-looking needle. Sam looked away, but Denzil took a step forward, his green eyes flashing and suspicious.

"You'll not stick that in him, Villain!" he hissed fiercely, to Mr Gump. "'Cos if you do, I'll turn you into – "

"It's all right, Denzil," said Travis, putting his hand on Denzil's shoulder. "It won't hurt Wimpy, much. And it'll make him better."

"How can he be better with a hole in him?" asked Denzil.

No one had an answer to that. Mr Gump filled the syringe with the cloudy liquid from the little bottle, and positioned the needle over the thick muscles of Wimpy's shoulder. Everyone looked away, except Denzil. Sam noticed that her mother was looking out of the window, sadly searching the skies. "I do wish my husband would come back," Mrs MacAllister sighed.

"Gone away, has he?" asked Mr Gump, withdrawing the needle from Wimpy's shoulder, gently massaging the injected muscle, and putting the syringe carefully away.

"He had to fly," said Travis.

"To Honolulu," said Denzil.

"Gone to Honolulu, eh?" Mr Gump repeated, frowning. "If he can afford a weekend in Honolulu, he can afford to pay my little account."

"I suppose there'll be another account, for all this

treatment for Wimpy," said Mrs MacAllister. "How much will this cost, Mr Gump?"

"Nothing, for my services," said the old man, tenderly spreading ointment on the burns on Wimpy's feet, then binding one of his front paws with a strip of soft gauze. Wimpy tried to lick the paw, but got Mr Gump's hand instead. Mr Gump fondled the bear's nose, lovingly.

"That's very kind of you," said Travis, crouching down to help Mr Gump bind up Wimpy's other paws. "Very generous."

"I said it'd cost nothing for *my* services," said Mr Gump, "but I said nothing about what the Ministry of Agriculture and Fisheries will charge."

"Ministry of Agriculture and Fisheries?" repeated Mrs MacAllister faintly.

Mr Gump nodded, and his eyebrows did a slight flutter. "That's right. I'm going to have to report this bear, I'm afraid. The Ministry must be notified about the importation of illegal animals – especially when they're not housed securely, and are a danger to themselves and members of the public."

Mrs MacAllister went white, but Travis said coolly: "I didn't think illegal animals bothered you, Mr Gump. Not since you've got one yourself. A nice little monkey, isn't it? You must be very fond of him; it'd be an awful shame to have him reported."

Mr Gump's eyebrows did a bigger flutter, and his face went red. He bent lower over Wimpy's paws, and was very slow over the bandaging.

"I didn't think you'd be the sort to smuggle animals

145

in," went on Travis. "How did you get him?"

"It's a female," said Mr Gump. "I was at some wharves a few years ago, watching a ship from Asia being unloaded. One of the sailors had the monkey. He was very harsh with her, obviously bored with her, and wishing he'd never got the animal in the first place. I couldn't stand the way he treated her, so I offered to buy her from him. Cost me a small fortune. Like Wimpy, she was sick and ill-treated. I looked after her, then couldn't bear the thought of handing her over to the proper authorities. So I kept her."

He used a sharp, curved instrument to clean Wimpy's teeth, and carefully treated his infected eye. When he stood up, the old man's face was its normal colour again, and he looked very calm and determined.

"Very well," Mr Gump said. "I won't report your bear if you don't report my monkey. But you've got to promise to take it to a zoo by Monday. It could be very dangerous, if it escaped."

"I promise it'll be gone by Monday night," said Mrs MacAllister.

Mr Gump picked up his bag. "I'll call again shortly with some food for the bear," he said, and left.

Denzil crouched down by Wimpy, and put his arms about the bear's neck. He whispered strange little words to him, which Sam couldn't quite hear. Wimpy lifted his head and pressed his snout against Denzil's neck, snuffling and dribbling down the red silk dress.

"He's going to get better!" Denzil said, his eyes shining. "Oh, Sam! We'll be able to take him for walks, and let him –"

"Actually, Denzil, there's something else you've got to do first," said Mrs MacAllister quietly, in her don't-argue-with-me voice. "You've got to bring back my husband. You've got to bring him back safely, with all his feathers on, and you've got to bring him in to land carefully and gently, so he doesn't hurt himself. And when you change him back into himself he's got to be calm and composed, not panic-stricken. And he must be truly himself, not changed in some way, or always wanting to be flying, or anything weird. I want him exactly as he was before."

Denzil gulped. The instructions sounded familiar, and he remembered Valvasor had given him similar directions when he told Denzil to turn Mother Gurtler's flying pigs back into ordinary pigs again. Only, with the pigs, there were village people with butterfly nets helping to catch them, and the pigs hadn't flown far. But how was he ever to find Mr MacAllister?

"There's one other little instruction, Denzil," said Mrs MacAllister. "I want him *now*." And she left the garage.

"Sam?" said Denzil. "Have you some parchment, and a quill, and ink?"

"I can give you some felt pens and some paper," said Sam. "Why? Do you have to write another spell?"

"No, said Denzil, nervously. "I need you to draw a plan, and show me how to get to Honolulu."

Denzil sat in Sam's tree-house and ate the peanut

butter and jam sandwich she had brought him. Three hours he had been up there, hiding from Mrs MacAllister. He'd chanted several spells, tried four Connecting-Words, and turned himself into a hawk and gone looking for Mr MacAllister. Nothing worked – not even the hawk idea, because he got frightened by a small aeroplane, and some boys had shot at him with toy bows and arrows. Now Denzil hid in the tree-house, and hoped Mrs MacAllister wouldn't find him. Sam sat with him, trying to cheer him up.

"She'll kill me, for sure," Denzil muttered, munching dolefully on the sandwich. "I'd have been better off staying home, and facing Valvasor and the three spinsters, and the man from the fair I stole Wimpy from. Does your lady mother hang villains?"

"You're not a villain," said Sam. "Well, you are, but you're a nice one. Anyway, Mum would never hurt anyone. She hardly ever gets mad. It's Dad who gets mad. Mum just gets headaches and has to lie down. That's what she's doing now. There must be something else you can try, Denzil. Could you turn Dad into something different, that we could find easily?"

"I could turn him into an elephant!" said Denzil eagerly, but he could see from Sam's face that that wasn't a good idea.

"A pigeon, maybe," suggested Sam. "A homing-pigeon. Then he'd just come home. Or you could turn him into a dog, and whistle him back."

"Not without his permission," sighed Denzil.

They heard voices down below on the drive, and

148

peered out of the tree-house window. Mr Gump had returned, carrying a large covered bowl. He was knocking on the house door, and Gran had gone to answer it. They went together into the garage, and Sam hoped Gran wouldn't get too big a fright when she saw the bear. She was glad, now, she'd told Gran everything.

"Let's go and watch," Sam said, starting to climb down the ladder from the tree-house to the lawn. "Mr Gump's feeding Wimpy."

But before they were even off the ladder, they noticed a large black falcon gliding down towards their back lawn.

"Dad!" screamed Sam, overjoyed. "He's back! Mum! Theresa! Travis! Come and see! Dad's back!"

The door of the house crashed open and Theresa rushed out, followed closely by Travis. Laughing with relief, they stood on the edge of the lawn with Sam and Denzil and watched the bird come in to land.

Mr MacAllister did look magnificent. His outstretched wings flashed blue-black in the sun, and his dark eyes shone. With perfect control that was wonderful to watch, he swooped and dived over the garden; soared, singing joyously, into the sun, and zoomed down again. His family cheered and clapped, until at last he made one final, glorious swoop, his wings outspread against the breeze, and made a perfect landing beside the vegetable garden.

Then, before anyone could move, and while Mr MacAllister was proudly preening his feathers, Joplin sprang from behind a cabbage – and got him!

149

12 "The Weirdest Goings-on!"

ran knelt by Mr Gump on the garage floor, and watched as he gently but firmly put some of the meat mixture into Wimpy's mouth.

"There, that'll put some strength into you, my dear one," crooned Mr Gump, stroking Wimpy's throat to help him swallow the unfamiliar food. He gave Wimpy another mouthful, but the bear spat it out, choking and snapping. With infinite patience Mr Gump tried again and again, and at last Wimpy took another mouthful. Then he took another, then sat up on his haunches and pressed his nose hard into the man's hand, sniffing and grunting and looking for more. Mr Gump put a pile of the meat on the floor, and Wimpy gobbled it up. Mr Gump praised him, stroking his snout and ears, and laughing softly when Wimpy licked the remains of the meat off his fingers.

"You're very good with animals, you know," said Gran, admiringly.

"I love them," said the old man, smiling at her.

Gran noticed how his eyes twinkled under the ferocious eyebrows, and his smile, the first she had seen, was warm and beautiful. "You ought to smile more often, you know," Gran murmured. "They call you Old Grumpy, around here. It's not a good title."

"Well, what else could you expect from them?" growled Mr Gump, and his eyebrows began to quiver. "They're not good neighbours. Always yelling and screaming, and roaring up and down the driveway in their broken-down old cars. At least they got rid of that blessed motor-bike. This used to be a quiet neighbourhood, before the MacAllisters got here."

"Listen to yourself!" said Gran, sternly. "There you go again! Life's too short to be spent grumbling."

"I'm not grumbling! I'm telling the truth!"

"Sounds like grumbling to me. When did you last tell someone something nice about themselves?"

"1936. My only friend was dying of polio, and I told him . . . Well, it doesn't matter what I told him. But I'm glad I did; he died an hour later."

"That's just my point," said Gran gently. "We never know when an angel's going to come and tell us it's our time to leave the planet. We could have lots of regrets, if we don't make the most of this life."

"I'm happy enough," Mr Gump said. "I've had a good life, a fulfilling one, with the animals."

At that moment Wimpy laid his head on Mr Gump's knee, sighed deeply, and fell into a contented snooze. From outside came the sound of people cheering and clapping, and Mr Gump sighed.

"See what I mean?" he said. "They should be reported for noise pollution. Animals don't make that ballyhoo all the time. They communicate quietly. They're loyal and dependable. They don't spring surprises on you, like stampeding through your garden and causing havoc."

"Elephants would," Gran pointed out, making the old man grin. "But I know what you mean, Mr Gump. I have this little theory about animals. I think they *do* talk to us. I used to take in stray cats. I couldn't bear to see them hungry or suffering. And they talked to me. I could tell instantly from their meows whether they were hungry, impatient, just saying hello, or simply needing some company. There was one cat I loved, called Kama, and he used to hear my thoughts. Many times when he was outside in the garden I'd watch him from my kitchen window, and I'd tell him in my mind that he was beautiful. And every time I looked at him and thought that, he'd come racing in for a cuddle, and rub his head against mine. He knew what I was thinking, Kama did. I haven't told anyone else that; they'd think I had lost my marbles."

"Your marbles are all rolling around just fine," said Mr Gump gruffly. "I think you're a very intuitive and perceptive woman. Brave, too. Not all old crones can walk into a garage, see a grizzly bear, and remain totally in control."

"I had been warned about the bear," smiled Gran. "And not too much of that 'old crone' stuff, either, thank you. I'm only seventy-eight."

"You're very well preserved," grinned Mr Gump.

"I'd have thought you weren't a day over sixty."

"Cheeky young rogue," she muttered, standing up, and groaning because her knee joints were stiff.

Slowly Mr Gump stood with her, and he moaned because his back ached.

"I've got just the stuff for creaky bones," said Gran, with a gleam in her eye. "It's called brandy. Would you like a little one with me?"

"I'd like that very much," said Mr Gump, putting the bowl of food by Wimpy's nose, so he could eat the rest when he woke up.

Suddenly there was a terrible scream from outside, and the sounds of people shouting. Gran and Mr Gump listened, startled. Several times they heard the name Joplin, and then Sam shrieked, "He'll kill Dad! Stop him, Denzil! Do something!"

"I thought Mr MacAllister was in Honolulu," said Mr Gump, puzzled.

"Obviously he didn't make it that far," muttered Gran, hobbling over to the window and peering out. "There's something going on over by the vegetable garden," she added. "I can't quite see what it is."

Then she saw Sam rushing over towards the garage, carrying an upset and dishevelled bird. "I think your veterinary services might be needed again, dear man," she said, turning and smiling at Mr Gump.

Sam burst into the garage, and thrust the bird at Mr Gump. "You've got to save him!" she cried.

Mr Gump took the falcon in his large, wrinkled hands, and placed it gently on the work bench at the back of the garage. Talking quietly, he examined it thoroughly. "It's only lost a few tail feathers, I think," said Mr Gump, lifting the falcon's tail and investigating it closely. The bird twisted its head up to watch him, its beady eyes full of rage and indignation.

"It'll be all right?" asked Sam anxiously. "Are you sure there's nothing else wrong with it?"

"Positive," said Mr Gump, smiling kindly at her. "There are no punctures from the cat's teeth, no broken bones, no damaged feathers. I think I can quite safely say the only thing wounded is the bird's pride."

"That'd be right," grinned Travis, from behind Sam. He was there watching, with everyone else. Fortunately Mrs MacAllister was still inside, resting.

The bird began to flutter and squawk, and Mr Gump picked it up and carried it over to the garage door. Then, before anyone could stop him, he lifted it high above his head, opened his hands, and set it free. It leaped up into the air and flapped away over the old pine where Sam's tree-house was.

Immediately, there was pandemonium. Everyone raced out of the garage, fighting to be first out of the door. Sam and Theresa were both screaming. The little Chinese Emperor bolted across the lawn waving his arms, his red robe flapping strangely about him, and turning dark. Quickly, Travis slammed the garage door shut, and stood in front of the window so Mr Gump couldn't see whatever was happening outside. But the old man stared suspiciously past him, muttering something about the strange costume the boy was wearing now. "Good Lord! He's defying gravity!" breathed Mr Gump, his eyes popping, his eyebrows in a frenzy.

Travis put his arm about the old man's neck and hustled him over to Wimpy. "I see you've managed to get him to eat," he said. "That's really great, Mr Gump."

"It's spectacular!" said Mr Gump, craning around to see out of the window. But he saw nothing save two birds flying together in the sky.

"The weirdest goings-on!" Mr Gump muttered, turning pale and wiping his hand over his face. His fingers were trembling. "I could have sworn . . . "

Gran came back into the garage, and took the old man by the arm. "I think we should go and have that little drink," she said, and led him away into the house.

Things were quiet in the garden for a while, while the rest of the family watched Denzil and Mr MacAllister flying in the sky. Joplin sat with his back to them all, coolly washing tiny black feathers from his whiskers, and pretending he didn't care about losing the finest catch of his life. And that catch, having been rescued from the jaws of death and released once more to the wide safety of the heavens, was most unwilling to come down again. It just wheeled and shrieked in the sky, ignoring the smaller bird that pestered it.

Mrs MacAllister came out, looking tired and pale. She had been crying. She saw them watching the two birds, and Sam explained everything that happened.

Travis shook his head when she started on the bit about Joplin catching her father, but Mrs MacAllister took it remarkably well. "And now Denzil's trying to get Dad to come back," Sam finished, shielding her eyes from the sun, and watching the two black dots flashing high in the blue.

"It's too late, I know it is," whispered Mrs MacAllister, covering her face with her hands. "He's a bird now. He'll never want to be earth-bound again. I've lost him."

But at last the two birds began to glide earthwards, and Sam grabbed Joplin and held him firmly in her arms. Everyone breathed huge sighs of relief as finally Mr MacAllister and Denzil came lower and lower, and made brilliant landings right by the house. In a few seconds Denzil was himself again. Mr MacAllister, however, took a little longer to become himself. He gradually increased in size, his feathers melted into fabric again, his claws into feet, and out of his fierce bird-face emerged a human face, familiar and loved and bewildered. Then he was all himself, standing slightly hunched and looking lost. He noticed his family staring at him, and frowned.

"What are you lot gawking at?" he asked. "Isn't a man allowed to ... to ... Ah ... " he scratched his head, and gave his wife an embarrassed little smile. "What was I doing out here, love?" he asked.

"Just stretching your wings in the fresh air," she said, going over to him and putting her arms around him. "I do love you, you great wonderful goose," she added, crying while she hid her face against his shoulder.

"Falcon," said Denzil, "he was a falcon, not a goose."

Fortunately Mr MacAllister ignored him. He hugged his wife hard, and kissed her. "What brought all this on?" he asked, smiling. "Anyone would think you hadn't seen me for a week. I've only been . . . only been . . . um . . . Never mind." He looked over her bright curls at the sky. "I haven't felt so wonderful in ages," he said. "Look at the colour of that sky, love. Isn't it glorious? The world's so crystal-clear, so shining. I feel . . . renewed, somehow. Lucky to be alive. It's a wonderful world, isn't it?"

"It is now," she said, kissing him.

"Honestly, you two!" groaned Theresa. "You're too old for that!" She went back into the house, and the others followed her.

They found Gran and Mr Gump sitting at the kitchen table laughing quietly together over a secret joke. Their heads were close, their white hair mingling, and Mr Gump had a hand over Gran's. A half-empty bottle of brandy was between them, and Mr Gump was about to fill their glasses again.

"Oh no – not you two as well!" cried Theresa. "It's not even Valentine's Day, any more! I'm going for a walk." But she changed into her best jeans and new shirt, combed her hair and put on some make-up, and made a phone call before she left.

Sam and Denzil went into the lounge, and Sam flopped into a chair with Joplin in her arms. "Do you want to see a video?" she asked. "Travis would get us

157

one."

Denzil's face lit up. "Can we see the knights fighting in the galaxy again?"

Travis came in, and turned the TV on. "I'll just catch the news update," he said, "then I'll borrow Mum's car and we'll go out somewhere, if you like. Where would you like to go?"

"To the baths," said Sam.

"The galaxy," said Denzil.

"I don't think Mum's car would make it to the galaxy," said Travis. "Not fast enough."

Denzil's face fell.

Mr and Mrs MacAllister came in, and sat down together on the sofa. "Now that the bear's on the mend," said Mr MacAllister, "how about we all go and take a look at that new zoo that's been advertised in the paper? It's only an hour's drive away. If it seems like a good place, tomorrow I'll borrow a truck and we'll take Wimpy there. I don't know quite how we'll explain him to the zoo people, but I'm sure they wouldn't turn down a free grizzly."

"I want to go to the galaxy," said Denzil, stubbornly sticking out his chin.

"You can," said Mr MacAllister, "just as soon as we've delivered your bear to the zoo. Then we'll drive out to the museum, poke you into a cannon, and shoot you off."

"Will you?" cried Denzil, thrilled, wringing his hands and almost crying with joy. "Will you, Mr Mac?"

"He's teasing, dear," said Mrs MacAllister. "But

we're serious about Wimpy. We won't keep him here. And now that we know he's going to get better, we really need to look for a home for him."

Mr MacAllister peered at the TV, his face puzzled and astonished. "You know," he said quietly, his voice shaking with excitement, "I could swear that picture's clearer than it's been for months."

Just then the news came on the TV, and Travis turned up the sound. Sam sighed. "Boring," she said. But the first item was about their own city, Londfield, and it showed a little girl holding a photograph of her cat, and crying. Sam leaned forward. There flashed on to the screen a picture of a large room full of cages of animals, and some people in white coats leaning over a dog doing something to it.

"I think we'll turn it off," said Travis, standing up.

"Leave it on," said Sam, holding Joplin closer to her. "I want to see it."

Travis hesitated. The news reader said something about the Londfield University, and the animal experiments being carried out there. They showed the university from a helicopter, and Sam saw the long driveway with its rows of trees, the artificial lake, and the high red brick buildings. The camera honed in on a narrow building with a grey slate roof, which was the laboratory.

"The Londfield University," said the news reader, "is said to have paid large amounts of money for the stolen pets. The University spokesperson, Miss Leonie Pryde, denies that the University knowingly buys stolen animals, and says that the rumours are

159

spread by misguided and malicious anti-vivisectionists. However, five missing pets have been traced to the University lab, and have since been returned to their owners. Others have not been so fortunate. Two families have been told that their dogs died during the testing of new drugs for heart disease. While the controversy continues, people are advised to keep their pets secure at all times –"

Travis turned the sound down on the TV, and there was a long silence. Then Sam said in a small voice, "They're using the stolen pets for experiments, aren't they?"

"I'm afraid so, darling," said Mr MacAllister, sitting by her, and putting his arm around her. "At least, it seems that way."

"But that's awful, Dad!" she wept. "It's cruel! The animals suffer, and it's all for nothing!"

"What's an experiment?" asked Denzil, totally mystified.

"New medicines are tried out first on animals, to see whether or not they work properly," explained Travis. "But first the scientists have to give the animals the diseases they're making the drugs for, otherwise they won't know whether the drugs cure them or not. And sometimes the drugs work, and the animals get better, and the scientists know the drugs are safe for people. And sometimes the drugs don't work, and the animals die."

"But people aren't animals!" cried Sam. "Just because something makes a *rat* better, doesn't mean it works for *people!*"

"I know, Sam," sighed Travis. "That's one of the big difficulties with it."

Denzil sat biting his nails, not really understanding what all the fuss was about, but knowing that Sam was very upset about something. "That castle," he said, studying the aerial view of the laboratory, "is that where people do things to animals, like the men at the fair did to Wimpy?"

"Not quite the same, Denzil," said Travis, "but almost."

Denzil's eyes gleamed, but he said no more.

Sam sobbed quietly, and her father patted her back and stroked her hair. "New drugs have to be tested on something, Sam," he murmured. "Usually only rats and mice are used. There's a fuss at the moment because there's a group of criminals who are stealing people's pets, and selling them to the university for experiments. Somehow using people's pets is a lot worse than using rats."

"Murgatroyd's a rat!" wailed Sam. "And he's my *friend*!"

Her father sighed. "I know it's an awful business, love. But the animals don't suffer for nothing. Those drugs being tested at the lab – they're to help people with heart problems. Maybe one of the drugs they tested will one day help Gran, maybe even save her from dying. I know it's awful to use animals, but wouldn't you rather have a rat die, than Gran? Isn't it worth the death of one animal, to save human beings?"

"No!" said Sam fiercely, sobbing. "And it's not just

161

one animal. They had cages and cages of them. I love Gran, but I bet she wouldn't want Joplin to die just so she could have some medicine."

"Me, have some medicine?" said Gran cheerfully, coming in. "I've got the most wonderful medicine. I've taken it only a couple of times, and I feel like a new being. It's absolutely miraculous." She sat in a chair near Sam, pushed her glasses up her nose, and picked up her knitting.

"What medicine's that, Mum?" asked Mrs MacAllister, anxiously. "It's not something you found in the bathroom cupboard, is it? We keep Joplin's worming pills and all sorts of things, in there."

"Oh, it's not worming pills," smiled Gran. "It's . . . um . . . hag taper, I think she called it."

"Who?" asked Mr MacAllister, suspiciously. "Who called it hag taper?"

"Actually," said Gran, clearing her throat, and fossicking around in her knitting basket for the pattern book, "actually, it was given to me by an angel."

Mr MacAllister guffawed. "Ha! An angel! I don't know what pills you're taking, Mum – but they give you wonderful hallucinations. I wouldn't mind trying one of them, myself! I could do with an angel, to sort out the havoc this household is in at the moment."

"You may laugh on the other side of your face one day, my son," warned Gran, shaking a knitting needle at him. She added, looking at Mrs MacAllister, "by the way, I've invited Archibald to dinner tonight. You don't mind, do you?"

"Archibald?" asked Mrs MacAllister. "Who's Archibald?"

"Archibald Gump," said Gran, two spots of pink appearing in her cheeks. "He's gone home now, but he's coming back later to check up on the bear. I think you'll like him, once you get to know him."

"You know about the bear?" cried Mrs MacAllister, alarmed.

"Of course," said Gran calmly. "You don't really think anyone could live in this house and not notice your grizzly bear, do you?"

Mrs MacAllister shook her head in amazement. "It's a miracle you haven't had twenty heart attacks already, this weekend," she said.

"I told you. My new medicine is working wonders," said Gran.

Sam asked, "Gran, if an animal died so scientists could make new pills for your heart, would you take them?"

Gran thought very carefully, while she added some more stitches into her knitting. "Actually, I suppose all the pills I've been taking have been tested on animals at some time or other," she replied thoughtfully. "But don't worry, sweetheart, I don't take those silly old pills any more."

"Mum!" cried Mrs MacAllister, horrified. "You can't just stop your treatment! Not without medical advice!"

"I've had advice from a far Higher Establishment," said Gran, firmly. "I've flushed my old pills down the toilet, and I'm taking some new medicine. It's far

163

better than anything the doctor's ever given me." She added, with a sweet smile at Sam, "And I *know* it was never tested on animals. One day, maybe, all medicines will be like that."

"You've done something very silly, Mum," said Mr MacAllister, standing up. "I'm going to call your doctor, and tell him to come around immediately and talk some sense into you. I'm not having you throwing a heart attack, on top of every other disaster we've had."

He started to leave the room. Behind him, everyone started to snigger, then to laugh. Mr MacAllister felt suddenly uncomfortable, and stopped. He felt cool air where he hadn't felt it before, and had an awful feeling there was something wrong. Behind him, Sam and Denzil gurgled helplessly, then broke into mad hoots of laughter. Gran chortled, and Mrs MacAllister giggled like a school-girl.

"Well, what is it?" Mr MacAllister asked, turning around and facing them again. "I don't see anything funny."

"No, you can't," chuckled Gran, tears of laughter streaming down her face.

Sam tried to tell him something, but couldn't, and she and Denzil fell against each other, crowing with laughter.

Mr MacAllister snorted and rolled his eyes heavenwards as if they were all mad, and went out to check himself in the mirror. They all screeched with laughter as he turned around to leave the room; for there, in the same place where Joplin had torn out the tail-feathers when Mr MacAllister was a falcon, was a great big tear in the seat of his pants, and a pale bare bottom shining through.

After a while Mr MacAllister came back wearing different trousers. Everyone was still laughing, and he flushed deeply as he sat down. "I do not consider that at all amusing," he said with great dignity.

Still chortling, Sam and Denzil left to go and see Wimpy.

Mr MacAllister glared at Travis and the two women. "No doubt that was Denzil's trick," he said, huffily. "Well, you're not to encourage him any more. From now on we're going to have a bit of sanity and rationality around here. No more fancy tricks. No more optical illusions. No more surprises. Just calm common sense, and –"

At that moment there was a brilliant flash of light, and the air filled with a strange, shifting silver mist. The mists cleared, and an old woman stood in the middle of the room. She looked flustered and dishevelled, with leaves and twigs tangled in her smoky grey hair, and she wore peculiar clothes stained with dust as if she had travelled impossible distances. Shocked, she blinked at the people in front of her, then scratched her whiskery chin. "God a-mercy, I've done it again!" she croaked.

Mrs MacAllister fainted, and fell across her husband's lap. He didn't notice; he was stunned, speechless, his eyes fixed with terror on the apparition in front of him.

Travis too was afraid, but stronger than the fear

165

was his sense of amazement, and the suspicion that the other-worldly visitor was someone to do with Denzil. He glanced at Gran, worried that her sick heart would not stand such awesome astonishments; but Gran was still quietly knitting, and smiling fondly over her glasses at the newcomer.

"Wrong place again, my dear?" Gran asked.

The visitor looked sheepish and shook her head, clucking like a worried chicken. "My landings used to be more accurate," she confessed, "but it seems my remedies still hit the right mark. You're looking much improved, madam."

"I am, thank you," said Gran.

"Ah, 'tis good to hear," said the visitor. Then, in a sound like a thunderclap, she vanished.

Mr MacAllister collapsed back against the sofa, absent-mindedly stroking his wife's hair as she lay unconscious across his lap. "What in heaven's name was *that*?" he gasped.

"That," said Gran serenely, "was my angel."

13 Good News and Bad News

In the garage, Sam and Denzil were laughing as Wimpy shambled happily about the garage sniffing at everything he found. He stayed a long time around the place where he had spilled all Mr MacAllister's home brew, disappointed that there wasn't a drop there now. He had cleaned up all the food in the bowl Mr Gump had left, and when Sam and Denzil went to him, he pushed his nose into their hands, looking for more food.

Denzil bent down and hugged Wimpy's neck, murmuring sing-song words into his fur. Sam watched, almost crying with joy. "Oh, Denzil," she said, "he's going to be all right. All we have to do now is find somewhere for him to live."

"He's living here," said Denzil, standing up and confronting her. "He's my bear, and he's staying with me."

"He can't. We can't keep him, Denzil. He's too big, and he's going to get bigger. He has to go. We'll take him to that zoo Dad told us about."

Denzil's chin jutted out, and his eyes glittered dangerously. Sam clenched her fists. "You change my hair again," she said, "and I'll rearrange your face."

Suddenly light flashed through the garage, and Mother Wyse stood in front of them, looking more dishevelled than ever. Her hair had gone haywire, tumbling about her face like jumbled straw, and her eyes were just two bright spots behind the grey. Her clothes were dirty and bedraggled, and she looked windblown and confused.

Muddled and muttering, she dusted off her skirts, lifted her hair out of her eyes, and peered about. She saw Wimpy, and cackled with delight. Next she saw the MacAllisters' shiny red car, and she leapt back a pace or two, alarmed. Then she saw Sam.

"Ah – there you be, Agapantha!" she cried, her old face wrinkling into a triumphant smile. "Found you, at last! I wish you wouldn't keep moving, dear." Then she noticed Denzil, and her smile vanished. "Oh, you wicked boy, Weasel!" she clucked, bobbing her head up and down, and shaking clouds of dust and leaves out of her hair. "I've been to all sorts of bother, for you! All the way here, then all the way back again, then here again, then back to Valvasor's, then out to the far side of the Great Wood, and back here again. I'm getting too old for all this to-ing and fro-ing, you know. It's ruining my hairdo."

Denzil stuck out his chin and was about to say something rude, when Mother Wyse went on: "Well, 'tis no matter. I'm here now, and with a message from your master."

Denzil's face went white, and he swallowed noisily. "From Valvasor?"

"Of course it's from Valvasor! He's your master, isn't he?"

"Nay," said Denzil, doubtfully. "He exterminated me."

"Rubbish! 'Twould go against all his principles. Mind you, I wouldn't blame him for being tempted, after all the trouble you've put him to. He's in mortal danger now, thanks to you. Mortal danger, and perils far worse than any other ominousness that's ever worried him! You mark my words! – there's a black storm brewing, and a veritable sword of Damocles hanging over his head, and dangerousness worse than a dragon's lair! In short, Weasel, he's got a bit of an emergency."

Denzil's face went a shade whiter, and he croaked, "Emergency?"

"Aye," old Mother Wyse went on, her voice quavering with emotion. "My oldest and dearest friend, the greatest wizard in all of Christendom, forced to flee for his life, and take refuge in the Great Wood, like a common thief and vagabond! My old heart bleeds for him. The shame! The injustice! The wrong! And all because of the three spinsters! Never – *never* in all my born days – did I think I'd see such a thing! And it's all your doing, lad! All your doing! The power you have, to create chaos and mayhem! I always told Valvasor you needed discipline! 'You're giving the boy too much, too fast!' I said to him. 'He doesn't stop to think – he's too headstrong! He'll misuse the magic, you wait and see!' And you have – you have! And look what's come of it!"

She stopped, breathing hard, and wringing her hands as if in despair.

Denzil stuck his chin out again, and his green eyes blazed in spite of the tears in them. "Well, he won't have to worry any more," he said, savagely. "He'll never see me again. I've finished with him."

Mother Wyse stared at him, horrified. "Diminished him?" she gasped.

"*I've finished with him!*" Denzil yelled. "He'll never see me again! Go back and tell him that – that his life can be happy and wonderful again, because he'll be rid of me!"

Suddenly old Mother Wyse shook her head, and tears glittered on her cheeks. "Oh, Weasel, my love," she murmured, "I can't do that! It would kill him, if he never saw you again! He wants you back. Now. Today. Seven hundred years ago, to be precise. He misses you, Weasel – misses you, and longs for you and loves you with all his heart!"

Denzil stared at her, not understanding. "But I thought – I thought he hated me!" he said. "I thought I caused him peril and danger and chaos and all that other stuff."

"Oh, you do," smiled Mother Wyse. "You're a perpetual worry to him. But he loves you more than anything else in the world."

"So I can go back?" asked Denzil.

"Of course, dearie! You and your bear. He wants you both."

170

"He knows about the bear?" squeaked Denzil, shocked.

"Oh yes," cackled Mother Wyse. "I told him everything Agapantha told me to! I even told him about your frizzy hair – though I must say it looks normal, to me. And when I told him there was going to be a right shakedown, and the three spinsters were out to get him and were going to poke out his eyes, he decided a little holiday might be sensible. He's gone to his cottage in the Great Wood. He said you could take the frizzy bear there with you, and you could let it go in the wildest part of the woods, and it would be safe. You would all be safe, until things settle down again in the village. But he's waiting for you, Weasel – counting the hours, he is, until he sees your face again."

A huge smile broke across Denzil's face, and he went over and gave Mother Wyse a big hug. He grinned at Sam over the old woman's shoulder, and Sam joined in the hug too. Wimpy decided he wasn't going to be left out, and gave a soft roar and raised himself up on his hind legs, putting his huge paws on their shoulders. But he was so heavy he tumbled them over, and they all rolled about on the garage floor, laughing. Denzil found himself with his arms around Wimpy's neck, and he hugged the bear tight. "We're going home, Wimpy," he said happily. "We're going home!"

Mother Wyse sat up in Wimpy's food bowl, and they all laughed again until their sides ached. Then Mother Wyse staggered to her feet, brushed down

171

her tumbled skirts and petticoats, and combed her chaotic hair with her fingers. "Do I look pleasing?" she asked anxiously. "I might call in to Valvasor on the way, to tell him all's well and to expect Denzil home soon."

"You look marvellous," said Sam, hugging her. "Absolutely marvellous. Thank you so much for helping, Mother Wyse. I don't know what we'd have done, without you."

Mother Wyse smiled her wonderful old one-toothed smile, and vanished.

Denzil stood with his arm about Wimpy's neck. The bear shoved its snout into one of the cups of Denzil's bras, found an apricot there, and munched it up. "I'll go and say farewell to your family," said Denzil. He was beaming, though there was a sadness in his smile. "I'll miss you, Sam."

"I'll miss you, too," she said. She went over to him and kissed his cheek.

Denzil blushed furiously. "Gawd – and with Valentine's Day long past!" he spluttered, making a fuss of wiping her kiss off his face, so she couldn't see his grin. Then he marched inside with Wimpy, to say goodbye to everyone.

They were in the kitchen getting lunch, and everyone gave loud cries of delight when they saw Wimpy. Only Joplin wasn't impressed, leaping in one almighty bound to the top of the fridge, where he perched with back arched, hissing and spitting his disapproval.

Everyone made a huge fuss of the bear, and

Wimpy grunted happily as he went from one person to the other, loving the attention and the warm feelings that came from these humans.

Only Mr MacAllister kept his distance, picking nervously at the bandage around his hand, and muttering about the bear being unreliable and dangerous.

Suddenly Wimpy smelled food, and he lumbered over to the table, rose up on his hind legs, planted one bandaged front paw firmly in the salad-bowl and the other in the butter, and poked his nose into the bowl of mayonnaise.

Everyone yelled at him, and Wimpy growled defiantly. With help from Travis, Denzil dragged Wimpy away from the food, leaving a trail of butter and bits of lettuce across the floor. Wimpy wiped the mayonnaise off his nose with his paw, licked his paw, then looked longingly at the table again. Denzil and Travis grabbed hold of him.

"He's going to be too much to cope with, now that he's better," observed Mr MacAllister, sitting down on the side of the table farthest from the bear. "I'm glad he's not my problem."

"I really don't think Wimpy should be in here, Denzil," said Mrs MacAllister, as Wimpy, still struggling to get back to the food, knocked over Joplin's food bowl and shot milk across the floor. "He must stay in the garage," Mrs MacAllister went on calmly, as Wimpy tried to run on the wet floor, slid ungracefully across the kitchen, and came to a shattering halt in the pantry. Containers toppled from the shelves, spilling cornflakes, sugar, custard powder, flour, and honey down across the bear. Wimpy thought he had landed in heaven. Grunting in ecstasy, he began the long, delicious process of licking himself clean.

There was a stunned silence. It seemed an appropriate time to make an exit, so Denzil hitched up his bras, cleared his throat, and announced in important tones, "I bid you all farewell. I'm going home now."

All eyes turned from the food-bespattered bear to the boy. Denzil grinned at their astonished faces. "I got a message from Valvasor," he said. "I'm not exterminated, after all. He wants me back. Can't wait to see me, in fact."

"That's wonderful, dear!" said Mrs MacAllister, hesitantly. "But will you be taking Wimpy with you?"

"Aye – unless you'd like him," said Denzil.

Mrs MacAllister looked again at the devastation in her pantry, and smiled a little as she shook her head. "I think it might be best if he goes with you," she said. "I'm sure Valvasor's better able to cope with Wimpy, than we are."

"I wish you'd got me to talk to Valvasor when he phoned you, Denzil," said Mr MacAllister. "We could have made arrangements to get that bear of yours back to the circus. What'll you do – stick him in a box and send him by removal van?"

Denzil looked aghast. "Nay – he'll not be caged again! We'll fly." He went over to Mr MacAllister, and held out his hand. "Can I have it, please?" he asked.

"Have what?" asked Mr MacAllister, looking blank. "A plane ticket? I'm not paying for one of those, Denzil – not for you and that bear. You'll need to hire a helicopter, and carry the bear in a special sling underneath, the way they do in Africa when they transport animals to game reserves. I'm sorry, lad, but Valvasor's going to pay for this lot. You've cost me enough, already. Phone him back, and get him to arrange it."

"Denzil hasn't cost you as much as you think," said Gran, with a little smile. "I had a word to Archibald, and he said you can forget that little account for the pool."

"Very generous of him," said Mr MacAllister. "But I'm still not paying for Denzil to fly home in a helicopter."

"It won't cost anything," said Denzil, "just as soon as I have it back."

"Have what back?" asked Mr MacAllister.

"My magic charm."

"The medallion you took off him, Dad," explained Sam. "I told you he couldn't go back without it."

Mr MacAllister felt in his trouser pocket. Then he felt in his other pocket. He looked in his shirt pocket, then took out his wallet, and looked through that. His face went red. "Give me a minute," he muttered, and went off to his bedroom. A long time later he came back.

"I'm sorry, Denzil," he said, going redder than ever. "I think I've lost it."

14 The Greatest Good

or a full minute Denzil stared at Mr MacAllister, unsure whether to believe him. "You're jesting, aren't you, sire?" he said at last, his green eyes narrowed and gleaming.

Mr MacAllister grinned sheepishly, and cleared his throat. "Well . . . um . . . actually, I'm not," he said. "I'm sorry, Denzil. I really am. I put the locket in my trouser pocket, and haven't seen it since. But don't worry – I'll buy you another one. I promise."

"But it won't have the mystical, magical qualities," pointed out Denzil.

"No . . . " said Mr MacAllister.

"Or Noah's hair in it," said Denzil.

"I could put some of *my* hair in it," offered Mr MacAllister helpfully.

Denzil shook his head. He started to tremble, and red waves of light came out from him.

"Denzil, there's no need to panic, dear," said Mrs MacAllister nervously. "I'm sure we'll find your magic charm. We're all just a bit touchy because we're hungry. I'll make us a nice lunch, and then we . . . " Her voice rose to a little wail as Denzil began, with deadly calm:

> *O greatest loss! O deepest grief!*
> *This cannot, will not, be ignored:*
> *For in that thing which you have lost,*
> *The secret power of Time lay stored.*
> *Within the circle, endless, true,*
> *Betwixt the silver and the gold,*
> *Lay Noah's hair, and timeless age,*
> *The Past and Present, time untold.*
> *All this you lost! O, tragic hour!*
> *O, crime beyond mere punishment!*
> *For this great loss to humankind,*
> *The deepest kind of banishment!*
> *Now hie you hence to farthest place*
> *Beyond –*

Travis suddenly rushed at Denzil, clapping his hand over Denzil's mouth. Denzil fought like a wild thing, biting and kicking, but Travis held him tight, even though he nearly lost his balance slithering on the wet floor.

"Cool it, Denzil!" he commanded. "You're not sending Dad anywhere! Now calm down!"

Denzil squirmed and raged, but Travis remained firm. At last Denzil gave up and lay sobbing, his face against Travis's chest. "I can't ever go back now!" he wept. "And Valvasor will kill me, for sure! That charm was his most precious thing in the world. Oh, saints preserve me! I'm doomed! I'm doomed!"

"You nearly had *me* doomed," said Mr MacAllister, with a worried laugh. "You're quite a good poet,

177

Denzil. And an excellent actor. I could have sworn you really were going to banish me to some terrible . . . " He shivered, and didn't finish.

Mrs MacAllister slipped her arm around her husband's waist. "I couldn't bear to lose you again," she said.

"Again?" he asked, chuckling. "I haven't been anywhere."

Denzil suddenly looked up, hope like a light on his face. "When you were flying!" he cried. "You must have lost it then!"

"Flying?" murmured Mr MacAllister, doubtfully. "When I was flying?"

"When you were a falcon! Where did you go?"

"I've got no idea what you're talking about, young man," said Mr MacAllister, sitting down and picking up the paper. "I'm getting tired of your games. I told you I'd buy you another locket, and you'll just have to be satisfied with that. Now go out and climb a tree, or something. I feel like some peace and quiet."

"But I could turn you into a falcon again!" said Denzil eagerly. "Then you could fly over the same places, and I'd make your eyesight extra good, so you could see anything shining on the ground!"

Mr MacAllister frowned as he studied an article in the paper. For the first time in many months he was not squinting at the print. "Talking of eyesight," he said, thoughtfully, "I could swear mine is perfect now."

"Falcon-sight," said Denzil. "You've got falcon-sight. I guess the magic didn't all wear off. I'd make it even better, next time. I promise. Will you let me?"

"What are you talking about, lad?" asked Mr MacAllister, suspiciously. "If this is another one of your tricks, I'm not interested. Why don't you go and help that bear lick itself clean? That should keep you quiet for a while."

Denzil glared at him, and went outside. Sam went with him, and they sat on the back step together. Denzil's face was hard and angry, and he was close to tears.

"Why don't you make a Finding-Spell?" asked Sam. "I'm sure there must be such things as Finding-Spells."

"There are."

"Well, why don't you make one?"

"Because they're complicated and take a long time, and I'd have to use it all the way between here and Honolulu."

"Dad didn't fly to Honolulu. Maybe the charm's just around here, somewhere."

A strange car pulled up in the driveway, driven by a young man Sam hadn't seen before. The car was stylish and dashing, and so was the driver. To Sam's surprise, Theresa was in the car. She sat for a while talking to the young man, and they laughed and sometimes kissed.

"She's finished with Adam," said Sam, sadly. "And her new boyfriend's awful. Look at him – all handsome and posh, with his swanky new car."

"All dandified and niminy-piminy," added Denzil.

"Turn him into a toad," said Sam.

"Can't, not without his permission."

Sam's eyes gleamed, and a wicked grin spread across her face. "There's something else you could do," she said, and whispered in Denzil's ear. He smiled and nodded. Moments later there was a scream from the car, and Theresa leapt out, shrieking about filthy beasts. The young man looked as if he were doing gymnastics in the car, trying to catch something. He gave up, got out, and tried to calm Theresa down.

"Go away!" she raged, shoving him off. "You know I hate those things! I told you! You did it deliberately, didn't you? Just to see what I'd –"

"I didn't! I don't know where it came from! I swear!"

"You do so! You don't have a thing like that in your car, and not know about it! You're a creep, Charles Prendergast. Just go away, and don't come back!"

"That'll be a pleasure!" he shouted, getting back into the car, slamming the door shut, and turning on the motor. He yelled out of the open window: "Anyway, I like my women sophisticated and cool!"

"Go and get yourself some new ones, then!" she shrieked. "Get fifty of them, for all I care! And I hope they're so cool they freeze your slimy lips off!"

Charles roared off down the driveway without checking behind him, and Sam bawled at the top of her lungs, "If you run over my cat, I'll kill you!"

The car tore off into the distance, and Theresa smoothed down her curls and came over to the back step.

"Hi," she said.

"Hi," said Sam and Denzil together.

Theresa wiped off her smudged lipstick, and wished her hands weren't shaking quite so much. "There was a monstrous rat in the car," she explained.

"We saw Charles," said Sam. "But why were you screaming?"

Theresa glared at her, then suddenly shrugged and gave a little laugh. "I meant a *real* rat, Sis," she said. "Though I suppose Charles is a bit of a rat, as well. He drives awfully fast, just showing off. He just doesn't care about hurting anyone. Not like . . . " Her voice trailed off, and she sighed as she stepped between Denzil and Sam on her way inside.

Mrs MacAllister poked her head out of the kitchen window, and called, "Sam, will you pick some parsley for me?"

Sam stood up. "Come and help," she said to Denzil.

He shook his head. "I'll sit here and try to think up a Finding-Spell. Picking herbs is women's work," he said, and dodged when she tried to box his ears.

In the vegetable garden Sam trod carefully between the rows of cabbages, broccoli, and lettuces, and picked a few stalks of parsley. As she was stepping back on to the lawn, she noticed a collection of feathers. Long and sleek, blue-black and shining, she recognised them for what they were – falcon's feathers. She picked them up. Attached to the feathers was a small scrap of material from the patch torn out of her father's trousers. The fabric was not

181

just attached to the feathers, but seemed to grow out of them, be a part of them, as if some magic had stopped halfway between bird and human stuff. Sam laughed softly to herself. Just then she noticed something else in the grass, on the edge of the garden and half hidden under a cabbage leaf. It was gold. Bending, she picked it up, her smile widening. She hid the thing in her hand, and went back to Denzil. He was sitting on the step looking worried again.

"I just made a Finding-Spell," she said, trying hard to keep a straight face. "It was one that Mother Wyse taught me."

"You!" he scoffed. "You couldn't make one that fast. Anyway, I didn't see you do it."

"I know. I wasn't here. I was flying to Honolulu."

Denzil laughed scornfully.

" I found this," said Sam.

And she placed into his outstretched hand the magic silver and gold medallion.

Denzil's mouth fell open. Very slowly he stood, and bowed low in front of her.

"Sam," he choked, "I honour you as a magic-maker equal in power and cleverness to myself. I honour your swiftness, your skill, your –"

"Just honour my sharp eyesight," she laughed. "I found it, Denzil, when I picked the parsley for Mum. It was by the garden, with the tail-feathers Joplin pulled out, and a bit of material from Dad's pants."

Denzil's admiration turned to embarrassment, and he gave her a lopsided grin. "Oh, well," he said, "you weren't doing magic at all. Just ordinary woman's work."

"*You'll* be doing woman's work," Sam said, snatching the medallion back again. "Before you go home, you've got to clean up that mess your bear made in our kitchen."

"Clean up?" he howled, the grin vanishing from his face. "*Me* clean up?" Then he stuck his chin out, hitched up his bras, and said defiantly: "Never, Sammy Snarly-britches! Never, in ten thousand, thousand years! You'll *never* make me do women's work!"

Denzil emptied the bucket of dirty water into the laundry tub, put the mop away, and went back to the kitchen.

"A beautiful job, Denzil," said Mrs MacAllister, thanking him. "My pantry's never looked so clean."

"I can go home now?" asked Denzil, putting his arm around Wimpy's neck. Wimpy was shining; he had been washed and brushed by Sam.

"I think you can go now, lad," said Mr MacAllister. "Are you sure you don't want lunch with us, first?"

"No, thanks," said Denzil. "Valvasor's sure to have made honey and hedgehog pie, for me. He knows I love that."

Mr MacAllister grinned, and gave Denzil a hug. "It was great to see you again, Denzil," he said. "You will come back one day, won't you? By yourself, though," he added, hurriedly.

"It's my turn now to go back to his place," said

Sam.

"Don't remind him of that, dear," whispered her mother. She added more loudly to Denzil, "Are you going to wear my red silk dress home?"

"You've got my slippers on, too, dear," Gran reminded him.

"And my bras," said Theresa.

Denzil kicked off the orange slippers with their big pink pompoms, but he lovingly stroked the red silk, and looked longingly at the bras around his waist. "I do like the little pouches for putting things," he said, poking his fists into them, and strutting around like a well-dressed lord. "Even Sir Godric doesn't have nice pouches like these."

"Oh, I suppose I could donate them," said Theresa, smiling. "I don't think they'd fit me any more, after all the apricots and things you've stuffed into them."

"They'd still fit around your waist," said Denzil, measuring her with his eyes.

"There's something I'll tell you about those things, one day when you're older," said Travis, going over to Denzil and hugging his neck. "In the meantime, don't try to make copies of them to sell in the village market-place. You'll have the kings of England marching off to war with cannonballs carried in their bras."

"They're not that big!" protested Theresa, hitting her brother over the head.

"I could magic up some big ones," said Denzil thoughtfully. "They would be good for cannonballs. I could make some for horses, too, and they could

184

carry hundreds." He thought it was a very good idea, and was hurt when everyone laughed.

Sam went over and gave Denzil a hug. "Are you leaving from here," she asked, "or do you want to go outside?"

"Here will do," said Denzil, pulling out a chair into the middle of the kitchen floor. He sat down and lifted the medallion that hung about his neck, slowly polishing the moon on the silver side. Wimpy sat on his haunches close to him, his nose across Denzil's knee. He was half asleep, full of wondrous food, and feeling fine. Denzil stroked the bear's nose. "Do you mind if I make you a stone for a little while, Wimpy?" he asked.

"I don't think you'd better watch, Mum," said Mrs MacAllister uneasily, to Gran. "This could be rather . . . unusual."

"I wouldn't miss this for worlds," said Gran, pushing her glasses up her nose, and sitting in a chair facing Denzil, as if she were at the movies. "I'm getting quite used to miracles, after my angel."

Mr MacAllister crossed his arms and leaned against the wall, trying to look nonchalant. "Well, Denzil young man," he said gruffly, "I suppose this is just another one of your fantastic illusions. Remember there's a career here in television for you, if you ever decide to be a professional magician. In the meantime, just make sure you go straight home, and don't drop in and bother anyone else on the way."

"I've got somewhere else to go, but I won't be there long," said Denzil.

"Where's that?" asked Sam, but Denzil only smiled and blew her a kiss.

Then, while they all watched, Denzil muttered the words that would take him through space and time to home. And woven into those words were powers to make Wimpy into stone for an hour, and himself into a falcon, swift and strong. A dark mist swirled about them, full of stars, snatches of forgotten songs, ancient voices, and the shining winds of timelessness; then he and Wimpy vanished.

"I hate it when he goes," whispered Sam, and Travis put his arm around her.

Gran sat staring at the place where Denzil and the bear had been. "You know," she murmured, after a while, "we have all just seen the mists between the worlds, where the windows are."

"Not mists, Gran," said Theresa. "As Adam would say, just clouds of molecules being rearranged."

"It's illusion," said Mr MacAllister, but he didn't sound very sure.

"I know it's magic," said Sam. Then she looked up at Travis. "Where do you think he's going, before he goes home?" she asked.

"I think I know where," said Travis, with a slow smile. "I bet there'll be something quite wonderful on the news tonight, Sam."

And there was.

Valvasor stood outside his little stone cottage in the Great Wood, and looked up at the patches of sky visible through the tree-tops. It was a fine, clear morning, though very cold, and the old wizard's breath made mists in the air. In front of him was a table carved roughly of logs, with a small bench either side for sitting on. On the rustic boards were set out a large hedgehog and honey pie, a wooden bowl of crab-apples, two pottery bowls of fresh goat's milk, and a platter of bread and cheese.

Beside the stone cottage a female goat was tethered, and several hens clucked about in the grass looking for grubs. From the cottage chimney rose a thin column of smoke, and sunlight danced in patches on the golden thatch. It was a peaceful scene, and the wizard looked content and tranquil as he waited, his eyes scanning the sky.

A bird appeared, flying straight and purposeful in the morning light, and Valvasor stood up very tall and still. "Denzil, son of my heart!" he whispered.

The bird wheeled in the sky above the forest clearing, then flew like an arrow down to the table and the one who waited there. Smiling, Valvasor watched as the creature stretched and grew, and the gleaming wings spread, cloak-like, on the grass, then rose and changed to shining silk the colour of the sun. Beak and claws became skin, and falcon-eyes evolved to Denzil-eyes, green and shining and full of joy. Then he was all himself, and he ran to Valvasor with a yell of sheer pleasure, and then they were hugging and laughing and both talking at once.

At last Valvasor drew away, and held Denzil's shoulders in his hands, looking at him.

"Two days you've been gone, my son," he said,

"and it seems like two long winters. What have you been doing, apart from finding yourself robes as grand as my ceremonial gown?"

The happiness faded from Denzil's face, and he gulped and licked his lips. "Promise you won't punish me, master?" he asked. "Or terminate me. Or doom me. Promise?"

"I promise," smiled Valvasor.

Denzil took a deep breath. "I put a spell on a bear," he said, "so I could save it from the fair. They made it dance on a hot plate, and its feet were burnt. I'm sorry, master. But I had to. I couldn't save it, without the magic. I'm sorry."

"Where is the bear now, my son?"

"Here, master." Denzil delved in the strange pouches he wore about his waist, and drew out a dark stone. With great care he placed it on the table. Then he glanced uneasily at Valvasor.

"There's more," he said, licking his lips again. "I magicked some more animals."

"And were they, too, at a fair?" asked Valvasor quietly.

Denzil shook his head. "No, master. They were in Sam's world, in a castle called University."

"These creatures, too, were forced to dance on hot plates?" asked Valvasor, stunned. "I was hoping such things were no longer done, in the far future!"

"No . . . not quite that, master," said Denzil, nervously. "Experiments. That's what they did."

Valvasor looked puzzled. "Well, you had best show me these creatures, my son," he said.

Out of his pouch Denzil took a handful of tiny white pebbles. He spread them slowly across the dark wood of the table, and they gleamed in the early morning sun. "White mice," he said. Then he took out a larger brown stone. "A dog," he explained. "And cats, and a few kittens." He emptied the pouches, tumbling stones across the table, until there were about thirty of them there.

Denzil divided them into groups. "These are rats," he said, "and this is another dog. These are rabbits. And this was a big monkey. It was really sick, master. A lot of them were poorly. We'll have to look after them before we find them homes or free them in the woods."

"And how long have we got before the magic wears off, and we must tend to these sick and wounded ones?" asked Valvasor.

Denzil squinted up at the sun, and frowned. He was mixed up, because time and seasons were different between his world and Sam's. "About as long as it takes me to sweep the stable out," he guessed.

"Time enough to eat our honey and hedgehog pie, then," said Valvasor.

Denzil nodded, and sat down.

Valvasor broke some bread, and cut himself a generous portion of pie. "Are you not hungry?" he asked, seeing that Denzil was sitting perfectly still, his hands clasped together on the table by the stones, his face white and anxious.

"You're not angry, master?" Denzil asked.

"Why should I be angry, my son?"

"You said I wasn't to magic any more animals! You said if I put my magic on an animal one more time, you'd exterminate me! You said – "

"What I said," said Valvasor, cutting a piece of pie for Denzil, "was that you must not again put magic on an animal for your own amusement or gain or selfish desire. I said magic was to be used in harmony with all living things, for their good and their peace."

The great wizard passed his hand over the stones, and the magic and life in them glowed under his shadow. "And these precious ones you saved," went on Valvasor, tenderly, "are they not bound in magic for their own good, for their harmony and their peace?"

"Aye, master, they are," said Denzil, his eyes shimmering.

"Then you have done nothing wrong, my son."

"So you're not wild with me?" asked Denzil.

"Wild?" the ancient wizard laughed, and it was like music in that still morning. "Wild? Denzil, I am proud of you. Your compassion and kindliness inspire only the greatest admiration. You're a perpetual wonder to me. A perpetual wonder."

Denzil puffed out his chest as he reached for a piece of honey and hedgehog pie.

"Thank you, master," he said, and his face went quite pink with pride.